D0406137

TEMPTATION HAD NEVER BEEN
HARDER TO RESIST

What was the matter with this household? Did no one follow the rules of decorum? The door closed, leaving him quite alone with Miss Edgewood and feeling quite uncomfortable.

Still, he would not back down. He was a vicar, after all, and she was a member of his parish and under his care. He would begin by offering her an olive branch.

"I thought you asked me to call," he said.

"That was Mrs. Stiles, I'm afraid," said Grace.

"I see. Well, that is neither here nor there. I have my own reason for coming. I thought I should beg your pardon for my boorish behavior last night." Aha! That took the wind out of her sails! And now that he was on her good side, perhaps she would listen to him.

But Grace only flashed him a militant glare and moved closer, taking the chair her uncle had just vacated.

"Very well, Mr. Havenhurst," she said. Did he detect the beginning of a smile? "I accept your apology, though I still do not know what you were doing outside the bathhouse so late last night."

And with that facer, she knocked him flat.

Also by Julia Parks

THE DEVIL AND MISS WEBSTER

Published by Zebra Books

HIS SAVING GRACE

Julia Parks

ZEBRA BOOKS
Kensington Publishing Corp.
http://www.kensingtonbooks.com

ZEBRA BOOKS are published by

Kensington Publishing Corp.
850 Third Avenue
New York, NY 10022

Copyright © 2002 by Donna Bell

All rights reserved. No part of this book may be reproduced
in any form or by any means without the prior written consent of the Publisher, excepting brief quotes used in reviews.

If you purchased this book without a cover you should be
aware that this book is stolen property. It was reported as
"unsold and destroyed" to the Publisher and neither the
Author nor the Publisher has received any payment for this
"stripped book."

All Kensington titles, imprints, and distributed lines are
available at special quantity discounts for bulk purchases for
sales promotion, premiums, fund-raising, educational or in-
stitutional use.

Special book excerpts or customized printings can also be
created to fit specific needs. For details, write or phone the
office of the Kensington Special Sales Manager: Kensington
Publishing Corp., 850 Third Avenue, New York, NY 10022.
Attn. Special Sales Department. Phone: 1-800-221-2647.

Zebra and the Z logo Reg. U.S. Pat. & TM Off.

First Printing: July 2002
10 9 8 7 6 5 4 3 2 1

Printed in the United States of America

For my new grandson,
Truman

One

"I believe you'll enjoy our little village, Vicar. I know it isn't London, but I think that's all to the good, as I'm sure you'll agree when you have had time to get to know everyone."

"I already like Pixley, Squire Lambert. I've seen one fox and three pheasants as I drove toward the village; it's good to know things haven't changed so very much since I was a boy and used to visit my father's hunting box," said the driver of the shiny black curricle, never hesitating as he turned the vehicle through the white wooden gate leading to his new home.

As they stopped and alighted, the squire remarked, "Of course, I forget about Foxworth belonging to your family; it's been used so little in the past few years."

"My brother is not terribly fond of fox hunting or for other wild game," said the Honorable Adam Havenhurst, carefully keeping his voice even to prevent the sarcasm from slipping through. His brother preferred hunting among the salons of London, but perhaps Alexander's reputation as a rake hadn't yet reached the wilds of Leichestershire, and as a vicar, he didn't wish to gossip.

"Well, well, one can hardly blame the Earl of Foxworth for that. I understand he has, uh, other interests," said the squire, taking a sudden interest in his waistcoat and tugging at it to make certain it was joining his breeches to keep his wide girth covered. Clearing his throat, he asked, "So you enjoy hunting, Mr. Havenhurst?"

As Adam made certain the brake was secure and went to the back of the curricle where he had lashed two large bandboxes, he replied, "Yes, I enjoy it immensely. My father always kept a pack of hounds, even in Sussex."

"I knew your father, hunted with him any number of times. Pixley owes him a great deal. Did you know that he put the new roof on the church? The old one fell in after a fire destroyed the south wall of the building. It's been twenty years now. I was just a youth, but I remember my father talking about it." With a flourish, the squire opened the front door and stood aside for the new vicar to pass by.

"No, I didn't know that, but I'm not surprised. He was a good man, very generous. Don't know how he ever managed to put up with my mother as long as he did," muttered the new vicar of Pixley, crossing the threshold into his new home and setting down his boxes.

The Honorable Adam Havenhurst's inspection of the abode, which took very little time due to the modest size of the vicarage, served to allow the squire time to pretend he hadn't heard the vicar's disparaging remark about his mother, the present dowager countess.

His hands clad in gloves of soft, buttery leather, Adam ran a finger along the narrow plank that served as a mantel and turned with a forced smile to say, "It is very neat and clean, I see."

Beaming, the squire rocked on his heels and said, "The ladies of the parish, my good wife included, have been toiling all week to make this place shine. They'll be tickled pink to know you approve."

Adam gave a regal nod and said, "Please thank them for me. Now, I think I should unpack and begin to settle in." He crossed the room in four strides and stood by the door, leaving the squire no choice but to follow.

"When will your servant arrive with your trunks?" asked the squire as he turned back to face the new vicar.

"Everything was in the boot of my carriage, and I'm afraid I don't have any servants. I suppose I should hire someone to cook and clean for me. Perhaps your good wife might help locate a suitable woman?"

"She will revel in the task!" exclaimed the squire, his round cheeks creased with another big smile. He poked at the vicar's ribs with his elbow and winked. "No one too young, of course. Wouldn't do to have the new vicar causing gossip when he's only just arrived."

Adam Havenhurst managed to smile, but too many years of privilege couldn't prevent one supercilious brow from rising in disdain. Oblivious to this, the squire gave the new vicar's hand a hearty shake and rolled down the front walk toward his horse, which had been tied to the back of the curricle.

When he was gone, Adam waited until the good man had mounted before he followed, climbing nimbly into the curricle and tooling it around the small house and into the tiny stable yard. He hopped to the ground and set about removing the harness from his chestnut gelding.

He led the horse into the only stall and returned to the curricle for the food he had purchased from last night's innkeeper. The gelding stamped his foot at the offering and gave his chiseled head a mighty shake before deigning to bury his velvety nose in the feed trough.

Adam stroked the arched neck and chuckled. "I know, Caesar, this is not at all what you are used to, but we must do our best to muddle through, to fit in with the villagers." He gave the glossy neck a final pat and walked to the end of the barn. He pulled the door, but the rusty hinges wouldn't budge. Grasping the worn wood with both hands, Adam gave it a mighty tug. The wood creaked, and the hinges groaned. Adam removed his coat and waistcoat which Weston had fitted to him personally. Then he redoubled his efforts, bound and determined that this barn door would not prevail. His own grunts mingled with the door's protests; suddenly, the wood gave way, splintering off the hinges and sending the handsome vicar careening backward until he lay sprawling in the dirt.

Grinding his teeth to prevent any unseemly curses from escaping his lips (curses which the barn and its pitiable door richly deserved, but which he, as vicar, could not freely employ), Adam was perplexed by the sound of tinkling laughter spilling across his modest stable yard.

Scrambling to his feet, he glared in the direction of the laughter and found a dozen pairs of eyes watching him. Dusting off his breeches, he executed a courtly bow, which sent the dozen girls into fresh gales of laughter.

"Shh! Girls, you must never laugh at the misfortunes of others."

Startled by the throaty tones, Adam looked beyond his pint-sized spectators to the owner of this intriguing voice. Standing in the shadow of the trees was a tall, red-haired beauty with laughing green eyes and a generous mouth. Just then the sun broke through the clouds, and he reassessed the hair color; there was only a hint of red, and in the afternoon sun, it glinted like gold. He could see nothing of her figure, hidden as she was by the young girls, but Adam instinctively straightened his cravat and tugged his waistcoat into place before moving toward his audience.

"Good morning, ladies," he said, sweeping another courtly bow.

The girls curtsied, as was fitting, but their leader remained still, her eyes widening a little, but otherwise, she did not react to this civility.

"Please allow me to introduce myself. I am Mr. Havenhurst, the new vicar," he said, his eyes never leaving the buxom blonde. Really, he thought, she would look more at home in a dairymaid's garb than in the conservative lavender gown she wore. A gown whose neck was entirely too high, his lascivious side commented before he forced it back, deep down inside. Heaven forfend, his thoughts were running just as his older brother's did.

"How do you do?" said the dairymaid. "I am Miss Edgewood, and these are some of my pupils."

Before he could reply, one of the girls stepped forward, stopping just before him and studying him with a fierce frown. Suddenly she nodded and said, "I know you, but you don't look anything like my guardian, the Earl of Foxworth."

Adam frowned likewise, but he remembered his new position and forced a smile to his lips, saying sweetly, "You must be one of the Misses, uh . . ."

"Heart," supplied the beauty.

"Yes, Miss Heart. My brother mentioned you and I have met your mother, of course. So you are—?"

Again she nodded, saying, "Yes, I am Abigail Heart. My sister Amanda is back at school practicing her pianoforte because she does not like going out-of-doors."

"I see," replied Adam, looking past the dark-haired girl to their teacher for assistance, but she was strangely silent.

"Yes, but that is the only matter in which we differ, I assure you. My sister and I are identical twins, you know."

"Yes, I do seem to recall, Miss uh . . ."

"Heart," she supplied, her frown returning. "You are

not at all like your brother, are you? Not only is he taller and quite dark, but he never forgets my name."

"That is quite enough, Abigail," declared the curvaceous blonde, belatedly coming to his rescue. "Apologize to Mr. Havenhurst, and then we shall go."

"I'm sorry, Mr. Havenhurst, though I'm sure you know I meant no offense," the young lady stated matter-of-factly.

With another quick curtsy from every girl, as well as a nod from the beauty, they disappeared through the hedges and into the woods that surrounded the back of the vicarage.

Adam couldn't prevent himself from pushing aside the greenery to watch their disorderly retreat, some of the girls skipping ahead while others lagged behind. They were hardly the organized convoy one usually witnessed when confronted by a group of schoolgirls out for a walk; there was nothing of that serpentine procession most school mistresses found *de rigueur*. Evidently Miss . . . whatever her name was, her teaching methods were as unorthodox as her manners.

Just then, he heard her distinctive voice lift in song, a raucous melody he had heard many times in taprooms and such. Shocked, Adam leaned forward to catch the ditty's licentious words. Chuckling, he shook his head and let the greenery fall when her unique lyrics floated back to his ears.

With its nuts as seeds, broad leaf trees,
Are the mighty mighty oak,
The maple and the pretty beech.
Deciduous all, leaves do fall.
But conifers, like spruce and pine . . .

Adam returned to the wreck of his barn as fat raindrops began to fall. Quickly, he hoisted the heavy door against the opening and nipped into the barn to search for tools just as the bottom fell out of the skies.

The dairymaid and her students would be getting very wet. He wished he had some means of rescuing them, but dismissed the idea as impossible; besides, he thought, the beauty had been pleased to leave him to the not-so-tender mercies of his brother's ward. He didn't owe her anything.

Adam glanced up to find Caesar watching him closely. "Yes, I know, such sentiments are hardly Christian of me, old boy, but you must admit, the thought of that beautiful blond lady with her gown plastered to her figure is hardly likely to distress me."

The horse replied with a snort. "Yes, yes, I know. That observation is hardly vicarlike either. Well, I warned you, this caring for a flock is going to be tricky business for a man who is more accustomed to luxury and dissipation. And you, my friend, you can already see that this parish with its austere little vicarage is likely to test our mettle. Still, it's better than the last stint. Being a curate in the middle of the city was hardly my cup of tea either."

Adam hefted a long, thick board into place against the frame of the stable door. He located a heavy hammer and a few rusty nails and set about securing the board in place. Before tackling the task of wresting the remainder of the splintered wood from the rusty hinges, he removed his driving gloves. By the time he had nailed the old hinges to the new door frame, his shirt was soaked with perspiration and his well-manicured nails were only a memory.

Standing back, Adam gave a grunt of satisfaction.

"What do you think, Caesar? Not bad for the spoiled son of an earl who never did an honest day's work. I guess I did learn a thing or two working in those gin houses in London." The horse swished his tale in appreciation. Adam pushed the door, cringing as it groaned in protest. Glancing around, he spied a small wooden bucket containing some vile brown goo.

"This should do the trick," he said to himself, dipping his hand into the grease and smearing it on the hinges. Slowly, the lubricant did its work, and the door opened without squeaking too loudly.

"That's one thing Alexander never did," he mumbled to himself. "Daresay he wouldn't have a clue as to how to repair a door."

Whistling, he darted across the small, muddy yard and into the house. He noticed the good ladies of the parish had laid a fire in the kitchen, and he set about lighting the wood. Glancing around the empty room, he pulled off his boots and then removed his soaked shirt and breeches, neatly arranging them on the back of two straight-backed chairs before backing up to the meager flames with a grateful sigh.

The two-day journey had been a long and taxing. First, there had been a broken axle. The repairs had set him back several hours, and his late arrival at the posting inn had necessitated him sharing his quarters with a large, snoring farmer. At least he had had his own bed. This day had gone more smoothly, despite the barn door and his brother's annoying ward, but he was weary and dirty . . . and hungry, he amended as his stomach growled.

Recalling the basket the squire's wife had sent, he left the warmth of the fire and scurried to the front door, where the basket nestled against his bandboxes. He ought to go and change; this was the country and people tended to drop by at any time. His stomach protested, and he picked up the basket, leaving the boxes where they lay.

Back in the kitchen, he threw his wet clothes to one side and dragged one chair closer to the fire before opening the prized basket. The top layer of fruit, eggs, and fresh-baked bread made his mouth begin to water. Bless the squire's wife for taking into account a poor bachelor's stomach, and he said a quick prayer of thanksgiving before breaking off a piece of the bread and sinking his teeth into it. Digging deeper, he discovered a block of cheese and a sausage. Like a starving man, he bit into the savory sausage, unwilling to leave the warmth of the fire to search the drawers for a knife. Then he heard a noise from the front parlor. Alerted in the nick of time, Adam darted up the back stairs to his tiny bedchamber just as the door to the kitchen opened.

"Mr. Havenhurst! Are you home? I've brought my good wife to meet you," called the squire.

"I'll be down shortly!" he called, wondering how on earth he was going to meet the squire's wife when all his clothes were downstairs. "If you'll just make yourselves comfortable in the parlor, I won't be long."

He waited a moment and then started cautiously down the stairs but stopped when he heard the distinct sounds of someone working in the kitchen. Defeated, he scurried back up to the Spartan room. It consisted of a decent-sized bed, another straight-backed chair, and a small table with a candlestick. Next to the window stood a dresser with a washbasin and a small mirror. In the corner was an armoire, his only hope.

Adam crossed the room and opened the wardrobe, where he discovered a suit of clothes. They were old-fashioned and smelled of damp, but evidently the former vicar had been close to his height, and the clothes would at least cover him decently.

As he donned the loose breeches, securing them with a scarlet cord that was holding back the striped bed curtains, a chill overtook him. The fleeting superstition that perhaps the departed vicar didn't like his best suit of clothes being appropriated was quickly dismissed. He pulled on the shirt, stuffing it into the black breeches. Then he added the coat, another black garment made of inferior cloth which the Honorable Adam Havenhurst would never have allowed to grace his body. He buttoned the coat to hide the scarlet cord and then turned his search to footwear.

Evidently, the last vicar had possessed feet that did not match his size, for the shoes he discovered in the far reaches of the cupboard were tiny. His brow beading with perspiration, Adam managed to shove his large feet into the small slippers. Running a hand through his disordered copper locks, he gave a grunt of satisfaction, and perhaps no small measure of pain, as he minced his way toward the door.

With a taut little smile, he greeted his benefactress, who was busily putting away the food from the basket. She turned at his words.

"How do you do, Mr. Havenhurst? I am delighted to meet you," she gushed while sweeping a curtsy that would have met with approval from the queen herself. "I have met your brother, in London, and I was thrilled when my husband told me the Earl of Foxworth's brother was going to be our new vicar."

"You are too kind, Mrs. Lambert. And I must thank you for the basket of food you sent over with your husband. I only sampled a couple of things, but they were wonderful," he added, eyeing the bread that remained on the kitchen table.

"Well, I would have invited you to our house for dinner tonight, but I knew you would be exhausted from your journey and would want to settle in."

"Very thoughtful of you," he said, groping for another vein of conversation.

He needn't have worried, for Mrs. Lambert was never at a loss for words. "Mr. Lambert is waiting for us in the parlor." She took his arm and ushered him into his parlor, where they discovered the squire leaning back in the only soft chair, with his eyes closed and his breaths coming in a regular, rasping rhythm.

The lady's mouth pursed, and she said sharply, "Mr. Lambert!"

"Oh, what? Pardon me, Mr. Havenhurst. I must have dozed off. As you can see, I've brought my good wife who wanted to let you know she has already located someone to take care of your house and cook for you."

"Goodness, yes, Mr. Havenhurst. I would have had Mrs. Odstock here today, but we were unsure whether you would decide to remain at the vicarage."

"Why would I not?" asked Adam, taking a cautious step into the room and hoping he didn't disgrace himself by falling flat on his face. His feet had gone completely numb.

Mrs. Lambert swept a hand around the tiny parlor, saying, "We thought it entirely possible that you would prefer to remove yourself to your brother's hunting box. This can hardly compare with the relative luxury you could enjoy at Foxworth. I mean, you must be accustomed to much more . . . comfortable surroundings than the vicarage has to offer."

"Perhaps, but you and the other ladies have done such a fine job, I think the vicarage is quite charming. But I really must see to my unpacking. If you'll excuse me?"

Adam took Mrs. Lambert's hand and placed it on his arm, escorting her to the front door where he turned her over to the squire, who had leapt to his feet and followed them.

"I look forward to meeting your Mrs. . . . uh . . ."

"Odstock," she said. "Are you certain there is nothing else you need tonight, Mr. Havenhurst?" asked the squire's good wife, her words catching airily in her throat as he bowed and kissed the back of her hand.

"No, you have provided everything I need. Thank you

again and good day," said Adam, waving cheerily until they were on their way.

With a whoosh, he closed the front door, groped his way to the chair recently vacated by the squire, and flopped down. Gingerly, he removed the undersized shoes and waited for the feeling to return to his feet. Grimacing as they began to throb, he hobbled to the front door and put on the latch. Limping into the kitchen, he stripped off the old coat and made his way outside to the pump. After filling the bucket with the icy well water, he shuffled back inside, latched the back door, and began to remove all his clothes.

An hour later, his lean body washed and clad in his silk dressing gown, and his appetite sated, Adam sat down in the chair the squire had found so comfortable. Heaving a sigh of contentment, his eyes drooped, and he fell into a deep sleep.

"May we be excused, Miss Edgewood?" asked Pamela Baxter when the maids had carried the last covers away.

"Yes, but, girls," said Grace, sending her sunny smile down the length of the long table, "remember that it is Wednesday and time to write those letters home."

"Yes, miss," came the chorus of replies from the twenty-four girls who lived at the school. There was a scraping of chairs, and the girls, aged ten to seventeen, tripped lightly out of the dining hall.

"I think I'll adjourn to my library," said the one masculine voice at the table. Rising easily, the round, silver-haired gentleman moved toward the door, pausing by his niece's chair.

"Shall I wake you at midnight, Uncle Rhodes?" asked Grace when he chucked her under the chin.

"Such a teaser you have grown into, my dear girl. What are we to do with her, Mrs. Stiles?" he asked the

other remaining occupant of the room, a middle-aged
spinster dressed in a brown gown fashionable two dec-
ades since.

"I suppose I will be forced to take her to task again,
Mr. Dodwell. I do my best, but . . ."

The trio shared a laugh at their familiar joke. Then,
as Margaret Stiles watched his retreat, Rhodes Dodwell
made his way to his study, leaving the two ladies to their
own devices. As usual, Grace forbore to tease her friend
about her feelings for the aging Rhodes. Tonight, however, Grace was lost in her own thoughts, and once
Rhodes was out of sight, Margaret turned to study her
young friend.

"You have been very quiet this evening, Grace."

"Hm. Just tired, I suppose. I didn't sleep very well
last night," she said, justifying the white lie by telling
herself that her distraction at dinner was nobody's business but her own.

"Odd, I would have thought after swimming so vig-
orously last night that you would have slept like a baby."

Grace's brow puckered and her eyes narrowed. "You
know, don't you?"

"Know what, my dear?" asked the older woman coyly.

"What did they tell you?" demanded Grace.

"Only that you met the new vicar," said Margaret
Stiles, smiling kindly on her companion.

"And so we did," said Grace with an unfeminine snort
of validation.

"I also was given to understand that you, for once in
your life, were struck absolutely dumb by the new vicar's
handsome face," said Mrs. Stiles with a girlish giggle.

"Who told you that?" demanded Grace, rounding on
her friend. "I wager it was that Abigail Heart, wasn't it!
As if she has anything to say to the matter. Why, her
behavior toward the poor man was absolutely reprehen-
sible." Grace sprang to her feet and paced the length of

the long dining hall before returning to frown down her tormentor.

"Actually, it was Pamela, and she concurred with your description of Abigail's conversation. What she couldn't fathom was why you allowed Abigail to go on and on without calling her down. I find I am rather curious about that myself," said Mrs. Stiles, patting the chair next to hers.

Grudgingly, Grace sat down, but she didn't speak.

Finally, Margaret Stiles prompted, "Is he as handsome as Pamela says he is?"

"I'm sure I didn't notice," said Grace, flushing to the roots of her strawberry blond hair. Never one to be miss-ish, Grace grinned and looked her older friend in the eye. With a laugh, she confessed, "He is absolutely god-like, Margaret! I swear, I have never seen the like."

Margaret Stiles let out a little squeak and leaned closer. "Oh, do tell. Is he at all as we thought he would be?"

"Not really. You know, we thought he would be dark like his brother, but he isn't. His hair is like copper, and his eyes are brown, rather like a doe, but very masculine, of course."

"Is he very tall and broad-shouldered?" Margaret sighed.

"Not so tall, perhaps an inch taller than I am, but those shoulders . . . everything a girl could hope for and more. He was working in the barn and had removed his coat and waistcoat, so there was very little left to the imagi-nation."

"Then he is nothing like the London dilettante we feared."

"No, nothing like that," said Grace, sitting back with a sigh and closing her eyes to picture once again the new vicar in his elegant shirt and snug breeches.

"Why, Grace Edgewood, if I didn't know your head

was so well attached, I would say you have fallen head over heels for our new vicar."

A lazy smile formed on Grace's generous mouth as she opened her bright green eyes and replied, "I think, Margaret, that you are very discerning."

"Grace, you've only just met the man!" exclaimed Mrs. Stiles, more than a little alarmed.

"Don't worry, Margaret, you know it will take more than a handsome face for me to lose my heart. The real test is yet to come. I think I'll go down to the bathhouse for a swim."

Grace rose in one smooth, lithe movement and strolled over to the door. There she paused and turned back for her parting shot. "But as a teacher, this is one test I am going to enjoy giving."

Margaret Stiles followed Grace out of the dining hall, but she detoured to the book-filled study, where Rhodes Dodwell preferred to pass his evenings. In truth, Mrs. Stiles looked for any excuse to breach this masculine bastion that was his study, and her news about the new vicar was certainly excuse enough.

"Oh, Mrs. Stiles, it's you. Won't you come in and be seated? I was hoping you would come. I am concerned about this invitation I have received from Mrs. Lambert. You know how she always wants to be the first hostess to entertain any new neighbors who venture into our little village, and here it is, brought over by one of her footmen."

"How delightful," said Margaret, already looking forward to seeing Grace with the new vicar.

"To be sure, but she has included on the invitation not only you, me, and Grace, but also the older girls. Do you think it proper of us to allow them to go without their parents' express permission? You know I defer to your wise judgment in all such matters of social protocol."

"You are too kind, Mr. Dodwell. Which girls has she included?"

"Pamela Baxter, Diana Cochran, and Olivia Wood."

"But that is understandable, Mr. Dodwell. Those are the girls closest to her own daughter Millie who was with us only last year. The three girls you mentioned are her best friends."

"True, I didn't look at it that way. Then you think we should allow them to attend?"

"This is a small country soiree. I can see no harm in it. Only Olivia's family might quibble about it since they are very conscious of their position in Society. When is the party?"

"Next week. On Thursday."

"Then we have time to send a message to Olivia's mother and ask her permission." Rising reluctantly, Mrs. Stiles added, "In the meanwhile, I will apprise the girls of this coming event and address the all-important issue of dress. They will have nothing suitable to wear and will need to take a day off from their lessons tomorrow to visit Mrs. Brough in the village."

"Oh, you ladies and your fashions," said the old bachelor. "I tell you what, Mrs. Stiles, while you are at the dressmaker's, order a new gown for yourself and see to it that my niece does the same, and have Mrs. Brough send all the bills to me. We mustn't forget that our little school is still in its infancy, and we must always strive to put on our best front to keep the approval of our neighbors."

"True," said Mrs. Stiles with a sigh. Then she brightened and added, "I do think, however, that we have managed to win over most of the village. I am very proud of our school here."

"As am I, but you must admit there are still parents

who look askance at our rather unusual curriculum. I myself had never heard of girls learning Greek and Latin, much less learning to swim."

"Oh, speaking of swimming, Grace has gone down to the bathhouse; I must check with her about the outing tomorrow before speaking to the girls."

As she hurried away, Rhodes Dodwell called after her, "And tell her I absolutely insist she order herself a new gown for the occasion!"

Grace slowed her pace, turning over so that she could stare at the tiled ceiling eighteen feet above her. One languid arm followed the other until she finally stilled, floating in one position, gazing upward, but instead of seeing the mortar and tile, she conjured up the new vicar in her mind's eye.

He was not all that handsome, she tried to convince herself, but even as the thought formed, she dismissed it. Grace Edgewood had never been in love, but she had seen others smitten with the ailment, and each one had been struck blind to all his lover's imperfections. She wasn't like that about the new vicar, so she couldn't possibly be in love. She had seen the flash of annoyance cross his dark eyes at Abigail's impertinence. She had noticed the forced quality of his smile and the tension in his deep voice. She had also felt his eyes travel the length of her torso as he studied her figure, something a truly perfect vicar would never have done. Yes, she had noticed all his faults.

She had to admit that his features were near to perfection, but the fact that she thought him merely *near* to perfection pointed out how clearly her thought processes were working. And he could certainly have used another inch or two of height. As it was, when they strolled arm in arm like the heroes and heroines of the novels she devoured, she would never fit under his arm.

No, she was thinking much too clearly to have fallen head over heels over the new vicar.

"Grace! Grace! Come here!"

Grace flipped over and swam quickly to the side of the large stone pool. "What is it, Margaret?"

"We have been invited to a soiree by Mrs. Lambert for next Thursday to get acquainted with the new vicar. She even included Pamela, Olivia, and Diana."

"Quite understandable. I believe Millie has come home from Bath where she was visiting with her aunt," said Grace.

"I told your uncle it would be all right for them to attend, even though they are still in the schoolroom. But what is more exciting is that your uncle insists we all have new gowns made up for the occasion."

"How wonderful!" exclaimed Grace, hoisting herself out of the warm water and onto the stone pavement that lined the floor of the great bathhouse, a task made more difficult by the heavy woolen bathing costume she wore.

"I thought we could take tomorrow morning and go into the village," said Margaret, surprised that Grace, who was usually so frugal with her wealthy uncle's pennies, hadn't given some sort of argument. Five gowns was quite an extravagance.

Her mouth dropped open when Grace continued. "An excellent idea! What time do you want to leave? Early, I should think, for there is bound to be a rush on Mrs. Brough's time when everyone in the parish receives their invitations."

"Yes, I will have Patrick ready the carriage right after breakfast," said Margaret, beginning to smile.

"Perfect." With this, Grace picked up a towel, wrapping it around her wet hair. When she had dried off and slipped into a thick flannel wrapper, she headed for the house, leaving her friend dumbfounded at the ease of her victory.

"Don't tell me you're not head over heels," muttered Mrs. Stiles as she followed Grace through the enclosed passageway that led to the house.

Two

Adam Havenhurst woke to a drizzling rain and cramped muscles. Sleeping in the chair had not been the wisest choice, he realized as he stood up, shivering from the morning chill and lack of cover. If the small clock with its cracked face on the mantel was correct, it was only five o'clock. Groaning, he climbed the stairs and sought his bed, finding a more peaceful rest and dreams seasoned with green eyes and short blond curls.

Growing up with four older brothers, if there was one lesson Grace had learned well, it was that when one didn't wish to cause a fuss, one rose early and cleared out of the house before anyone had a chance to fire the first volley of teasing questions. With this in mind, Grace left a carefully worded note for Mrs. Stiles, saying she had many errands in the village and would meet her and their three students at the dressmaker's at ten o'clock.

By seven o'clock, the rain had ceased, and the sun was making an effort to burn away the last clouds. As the girls and Mrs. Stiles were descending for breakfast, Grace was putting her horse to the first fence and disappearing from the view of Dodwell's Progressive Academy for Young Ladies. Another pasture swept by before she pulled back on the reins and slowed her bay gelding to a walk. Under an old oak, she lifted her right leg out of the upper pommel and slid to the ground. After hobbling Baldy, who tended to amble, she untied the knapsack secured to the saddle and pulled out two apples. Taking out her late father's pocketknife, she cut one apple into quarters and proceeded to feed them to Baldy, who accepted these as his due for having taken two jumps without balking.

"You know, Baldy, some people will call me bold for visiting the new vicar without a maid," she said, holding the second apple out of his reach as he butted his head against her chest for another piece. "No, this one is mine," she said, taking a bite, her brow furrowed.

"But I think it is simply the neighborly thing to do, don't you? I mean, the man probably doesn't have anything in his kitchen to eat, and even if he does, who's to say whether he knows how to cook or not."

She relented and gave another slice to the persistent beast.

"So really, to take him some of Cook's scones and some marmalade is the charitable thing to do."

Baldy was more than happy to agree when she fed him the remainder of her apple. Grace removed the hobbles and led him over to the old tree, whose lowest branches formed a vee for her climb onto the big horse's back, slipping her right leg in the upper pommel of her sidesaddle and settling her skirts to cover her ankles.

It was nearly eight o'clock when Grace slid to the ground again and looped the reins over the vicarage's gatepost.

In the quiet of the morning, she whispered to her horse, "No smoke from the chimneys. Surely the man's awake by now. Of course, it could mean he doesn't know how to cook."

Taking a deep breath, she grasped the knapsack and

headed for the front door, rapping firmly on it and standing back in anticipation.

Nothing. Grace turned to grimace at her horse before knocking again.

After a moment, she heard noises—bumping and thumping and a muffled oath. Though tempted to leave her offering on the doorstep, Grace stood her ground, straightening her shoulders and lifting her firm jaw as the door opened.

His dressing gown loosely tied, his feet bare, and his copper hair standing on end, Adam frowned mightily at his early caller. Then his brown eyes widened, and he said, "Oh, it's you. I thought . . . well, never mind. Won't you come in?"

As he moved aside for her to enter, he raked one hand through his hair, and arranged his dressing gown more securely. Stepping around her, the vicar led the way to the kitchen.

"I suppose you'll want to start in here," he said.

"Start?" asked Grace, puzzled by this turn in their conversation.

"Yes, I must confess I'm more than a little surprised to see you. After what the squire said about scandals and village gossip, I assumed you'd be much older and more matronly," he said, arriving in the tiny kitchen and turning to smile at her.

Cocking her head to one side, Grace frowned and shuffled from one foot to the other before holding out the knapsack.

"I thought you might be hungry," she said.

"Well, yes, but isn't that why you're here, Miss, uh . . . ?"

"Edgewood," she supplied, backing away.

"Yes, Miss Edgewood," began Adam, a cold dread creeping into his consciousness. "Wait a minute," he began.

Just then someone rattled the latch on the back door. Relieved to be saved from an awkward situation, the new vicar hurried to let the new visitor inside. It was a woman of sixty or seventy, her hair tied back under a spotted kerchief, and a mustache on her upper lip any youth would have been proud to sport.

"So you're the new vicar," she growled, studying him fiercely, her bushy brows coming together to form one.

"Why, yes, and you are . . . ?" He knew the answer even as he asked.

"Your housekeeper, Mrs. Odstock. Mrs. Lambert sent me to look after you." She turned her forceful glare on Grace and demanded, "What's she doing here? I don't serve in a house where that sort of thing goes on."

"Miss Edgewood? No, no, she, uh . . . that is . . ." He reached into the knapsack and produced a small pot containing something very sticky, grimacing as he pulled his thumb out of the jar. "She brought me some jelly," he said triumphantly.

"Marmalade," Grace corrected, backing toward the door to the parlor. "And some scones. If I had known Mrs. Odstock was coming to look after you, Mr. uh, Havenhurst, I wouldn't have bothered. Mrs. Odstock is well known for her scones and jellies. I'm glad to know you're going to be in such good hands," said Grace, turning to flee.

"And with me about, the good vicar has no need of charity from the likes of you, Miss Edgewood," said the crone, her voice rising so that her departing listener could catch every insulting tone.

Her face crimson, Grace fairly flew down the front walk and jerked the reins from the gatepost, sticking her booted foot into the low stone wall and throwing herself into the saddle.

As she whirled the gelding around and dug in her

heels, she heard a shouted, "Thank you for stopping by, Miss Edgewood."

Waving without turning around, she sped away, chanting to herself, "Stupid, stupid, stupid."

"Stupid, stupid, stupid," grumbled Adam as he watched her go before returning to the kitchen, where Mrs. Odstock had made herself at home, setting Grace's offerings on the table before putting on her apron.

In a daze, Adam sat down at the table and began slathering the first scone with the marmalade, taking a bite while he watched his new housekeeper disappear into the near-empty larder.

"I have the distinct impression you don't approve of Miss Edgewood," he said.

"It's not her; it's that school she runs. Too much learning isn't good for young girls. They'll all end up like her, thinking she's too good t' be a wife, an' that's what the good Lord put us women here for, isn't it, vicar?"

Adam murmured, "I suppose, but . . ."

She stomped out of the larder, saying gruffly, "There's naught but a broom and a few bottles of ale in there. If you want me to cook and clean for you, Vicar, I have got to have all the necessities to hand."

"Naturally, Mrs. Odstock. I'll visit the shops in the village today and let them know you'll be doing the shopping for me, if that's all right."

"Sounds about right," she grunted, disappearing again.

"If there's anything you need immediately, I could pick it up when I'm there today."

"There's lots I'll be needin', Vicar," she said, poking her head out and glaring at him. "You better get paper an' pen to write it down. In my experience with men, they never remember what they're told."

"Of course, I'll be back in a moment."

Adam disappeared upstairs, taking the time to run a comb through his hair and to put on his breeches and a fresh shirt. When he descended the stairs, it was to discover Mrs. Odstock picking up his discarded clothes from the previous night, her nose scrunched up in distaste as she held them at arm's length.

"First of all, we'll be needin' some soap. I don't have enough at my house to take care of the likes of this."

Adam hid a smile and sat down at the table, obediently recording every item she mentioned, one by one. By the time he had finished, his list covered both sides of the notepaper. He reflected that it was a good thing he was not a poor man, or he would never have been able to live up to Mrs. Odstock's level of comfort.

When he had harnessed Caesar to the curricle, she called out three more necessities she had forgotten.

"I shan't forget," he said.

"We shall see," she replied with a sneer.

Pulling back on the ribbons, Adam plucked up his courage and asked the question that had been plaguing him since making Mrs. Odstock's acquaintance not an hour since. "Are you planning to live here at the vicarage?"

With hands on her wide hips, the housekeeper's reply dripped with acid as she said, "And where might that be, Vicar? In th' hayloft or in your room?"

"Just so, Mrs. Odstock," he said, a sunny smile lighting his face as he tooled out of the stable yard and out of sight.

Grace's face burned every time she replayed the scene in her head, and that was practically continuous as she performed her errands. First, she stopped at Mr. Crane's shop and purchased more writing tablets and items Cook had requested. Then it was on to old Mr. Peabody's leather goods shop to leave her half-boots for repair, and finally she dropped into Miss Silverton's little emporium for the tobacco Uncle Rhodes couldn't live without and the French scented soap Mrs. Stiles adored.

Her thoughts of the handsome vicar exploded with new vigor at this last shop when he strolled through the door, removing his fashionable beaver hat when he spied the two ladies.

"Miss Edgewood, so nice to see you again. I must thank you for the offerings you brought over. Mrs. Odstock is just getting settled, and I'm afraid I would have starved without your scones and marmalade this morning," he said, smiling at her.

Grace flushed a ruddy color, and managed a strangled, "You are too kind."

Miss Silverton, a thirty-year-old spinster who still had aspirations of changing her marital status, cleared her throat.

"Oh, may I present the new vicar, Mr. Havenhurst," said Grace, the simple act of social courtesy covering her embarrassment. "Mr. Havenhurst, may I present Miss Silverton, who owns this shop."

"Delighted to meet you, sir, but it is the Honorable Mr. Havenhurst, Miss Edgewood," she said with a titter.

"Delighted to make your acquaintance, Miss Silverton," said the vicar. "I must say I was surprised and pleased to find an establishment carrying what some might consider luxury items."

"Oh, la, sir, you are too kind. What may I show you this morning?" gushed the bony spinster, circling the counter and closing in on her prey.

"Well, I don't wish to intrude. I'll wait my turn."

"No, no, Miss Edgewood was finished. Weren't you, dear?" she said, picking up Grace's small bundle and thrusting it into her hands.

"Yes, indeed. We had concluded our business. Good day, Mr. Havenhurst, Miss Silverton." Grace edged her way toward the door, but escape was not to be granted her as she felt strong fingers guiding her out the door.

"I'll be back in a moment, Miss Silverton," said the vicar, escorting Grace outside and closing the door behind him.

While he faced her, she could see Miss Silverton hurrying toward the windows, pretending to dust the display of teacups with a lace handkerchief as she strained to hear their conversation. It would have been laughable except that in Pixley, the favorite pastime of its inhabitants was gossip, and with her position as a schoolmistress, she didn't wish to give them fuel for the flame.

"I wanted to apologize for my error this morning, Miss Edgewood. I'm afraid I was half asleep when you called, and I mistook you for my new housekeeper. I knew better, but . . ."

"I assure you, Mr. Havenhurst, I haven't given it another thought," she whispered.

He leaned closer to hear her soft words, and said, "Nevertheless, I owe you an apology."

"Very well, I accept your apology."

"Good," he said, chuckling as he added, "I'm only sorry you aren't Mrs. Odstock. She is a very, uh, forceful female."

Grace smiled, the expression transforming her generous mouth into a warm and inviting place. The vicar swayed closer again until Grace's expression changed to alarm when Miss Silverton dropped her handkerchief and all pretense at dusting.

Stepping back, she said formally, "I'm sure Mrs. Odstock and you will get along famously, Mr. Havenhurst. Now, I really must go; I have an appointment in a few minutes, and I mustn't be late."

"Oh, certainly, only I have a little problem that I hoped you might help me with," he said, touching her arm. Grace waited expectantly but kept her distance. "Mrs.

Odstock has requested that I buy some soap. I noticed this shop, Miss . . ."

"Silverton's shop?"

"Yes, that's it. I'm terrible with names, I'm afraid. A lamentable fault for a vicar, I assure you. Anyway, I'm not quite sure this is the type of soap Mrs. Odstock requires."

"I daresay the soap she wants will not be found in Miss Silverton's shop, but it depends on what she wants it for."

"Well, I think she means to wash my . . . my clothes," he said, turning red.

Grace chuckled this time, her green eyes lighting with mischief as she said, "I doubt you want her to wash your things with perfumed soaps, although you may wish to purchase some sandalwood soap for your, uh, personal use. But for clothes, you would do better to go to Mr. Crane's shop. He has all manner of merchandise, including the soap Mrs. Odstock requires."

"Mr. Crane's shop, yes, I'll do that. Thank you again, Miss Edgewood."

"You're quite welcome, Mr. Havenhurst. Good day."

"Good day, Miss Edgewood," he murmured.

Grace could feel his eyes on her, and she couldn't resist the impulse to turn and smile. Her action caught the attention of the ever-vigilant Miss Silverton who had opened the door to her shop, and Grace blushed.

On the handsome vicar's face, the flash of a puzzled frown was followed by a grin, and he winked before turning and asking the shopkeeper politely, "Do you have any sandalwood soap, Miss Silverton?"

Grace Edgewood had an uncanny knack for selecting becoming fashions. She could look through the latest copy of *La Belle Assemblée* and tell at a glance which gowns would be the most pleasing. So when Mrs. Stiles and the girls began to ooh and ah over a particular engraving, they would then turn to Miss Edgewood for her pronouncement. Even the dressmaker, Mrs. Brough, usually deferred to her opinions.

Mrs. Brough was a talented seamstress, the widow of a wealthy merchant who had left her penniless by donating his fortune to his club. Since her sister was Mrs. Lambert, the squire's wife, she had moved to Pixley and set up her shop, which flourished. The countryside had never been so fashionable.

Under Mrs. Brough's supervision, her clerks brought out one bolt after another. Grace declared the sprig muslin embroidered with lemon yellow daffodils and red roses too colorful, while the one with sprigs of violets was pronounced a delightful complement to Pamela's fair hair. For Diana, who was so dark as to look almost like a Gypsy, Grace suggested that Mrs. Brough find a creamy silk to be trimmed with dark green ribbons. For Olivia, who had bright red hair and a tendency to freckle, they decided on a pale green, edging the neckline with tiny pink silk roses. The girls were led away by one of the clerks to be measured.

"That takes care of the young ladies, but what about you, Mrs. Stiles," said Mrs. Brough, who was already counting her profits with the rash of festivities the presence of a handsome new vicar was sure to produce.

"I would like something in dark gold, I think. You know, Grace, I have my brown, my black, and my blue gowns, but I don't have one in gold," said the older woman, fingering a watered silk in a brassy gold.

"That fabric is lovely, to be sure, but with your coloring, Margaret, I don't think it would be terribly appealing." At her friend's look of disappointment, Grace snapped her fingers and sailed across the room, moving aside lengths of cloth until she unearthed a piece in dark green *glacé* satin which she brought back for her friend's inspection.

"This is the one you need, Margaret. The color is perfect, and its lustrous sheen will show off your complexion."

"Oh, I like that. What do you think, Mrs. Brough?"

"As always, Miss Edgewood has an eye for color. We might trim it with a little of this gold. I could put a row of narrow ruching around the high waist and the sleeves."

"An excellent idea," said Grace, wandering off to look for just the right piece of cloth for her own new gown.

The cut of the gown had to be simple and elegant. She was too tall for rows of ribbons and laces. And the color should be . . . her eyes fell on a piece of mulberry tissue, more purple than red, shot through with gold metallic threads which she knew would complement her hair and coloring. She touched the cloth and it shimmered, even in the dim light of the shop.

"This is the one, Mrs. Brough. Short, capped sleeves—no puff. And simply cut, to the floor. You know how I like them."

"Of course, Miss Edgewood." She snapped her fingers and another apprentice hurried forward to take Mrs. Stiles in hand for measuring. Mrs. Brough tended to Grace personally.

"I saw you talking to the new vicar outside Miss Silverton's earlier. I was surprised you had already met him. He only arrived yesterday, I understand," said the dressmaker, throwing the tape around her hips.

"That's right, but I was taking some of my students out for a walk to study the trees, and we happened upon him. Do remember, Mrs. Brough, that the neckline cannot be too low."

"Certainly, miss. I know how you like it. Tell me,

what's he like. Handsome, I could tell just from looking, but is he very high in the instep?"

"I didn't notice really."

"Oh? Well, Mrs. Gray and I were discussing it the other day, wondering how he would be, the son of an earl and all. I told her I didn't know about this business of giving the living of our little parish to the son of the current Earl of Foxworth. He has such a wicked reputation, you know."

"No, coming from Hereford, I wasn't aware of his reputation, but I really don't see what that has to say to the matter. We have his brother for our vicar, not the earl, and he seems quite nice," said Grace, hoping her words would put an end to this uncomfortable vein of conversation.

Margaret appeared from the back room just then and saved her from any more of Mrs. Brough's speculations.

"I will take the girls back to the school as soon as we are finished unless there is something I can do to help you with your errands this morning, Grace."

"No, I've finished all my shopping. I told Mr. Crane to place everything in the carriage when he saw it outside Mrs. Brough's so that you could take it back to school. I only want to stop by Mrs. Lambert's and discuss our bringing the girls. I want her to know they will only be joining in on the country dances, not the waltzes."

"Oh, Miss Edgewood! Mr. Dodwell taught us the waltz, and we think it's lovely," said Pamela, the eldest of the three girls.

"Lovely, but still considered a little fast by some people, especially here in the country. You wouldn't wish to offend anyone; nor would you like for your parents to hear about it. You might not be allowed to attend the next ball."

"Yes, Miss Edgewood," said Pamela with a docile

smile. "We shall have fun anyway. I can't believe it! My very first ball!"

"I can hardly wait!" Diana sighed.

The three girls floated out the door, followed by a laughing Mrs. Stiles. After thanking Mrs. Brough for agreeing to make up the gowns so quickly, Grace also left, waving at the carriage as they pulled away from the shop.

Her horse was still in front of Mr. Crane's store, and through the open door she could see Mr. Havenhurst deep in conversation with the gossipy merchant. If the vicar spied her climbing onto Baldy, he was bound to engage her in another embarrassing exchange. That was all she needed, to become the topic of gossip along with the new vicar. It had only been in the past six months that they had ceased talking about the school's scandalous bathhouse!

With a snap of her fingers, Grace turned on her heel and headed in the opposite direction, turning into John Gray's blacksmithing shop.

"Good morning, Mr. Gray. I was wondering if you could take a look at Baldy's shoes. I think it might be time to replace them."

"O' course, Miss Edgewood," said the massive man, wiping his hands on his leather apron and looking around expectantly. "Where is he?"

"Oh, well, I had tethered him at Mr. Crane's, and thought I should check with you first, to see if you have the time, that is, and you do, so I'll . . . Is little John around?"

"No, he's gone to visit his granny."

They were at an impasse, it seemed. Reluctantly, Grace turned to retrieve her horse to have his perfectly fitting shoes checked for no reason.

"I need to go over to Mr. Crane's and pick up a bit of

liniment, so if you don't mind waitin', miss, I'll fetch Baldy back with me."

"Oh, that would be wonderful, and I'll just step up to the house and speak to your good wife."

"She'll be right pleased, miss."

The big man departed, and Grace, feeling secure and happy to have succeeded in her effort to steer clear of the new vicar, went up to the smithy's house, where Mrs. Gray regaled her with tales of all the rest of the village gossip.

She listened with only half an ear; from her vantage point facing the little window, she had a perfect view of Mr. Havenhurst talking to the shopkeeper and the blacksmith. His head uncovered, his copper waves flashed like fire in the sunlight. He smiled at something one of the other men said, and Grace's breath caught in her throat. Her efforts to put on an airy smile for Mrs. Gray fooled no one, and that good lady nearly broke her neck craning to discover the cause of her guest's distraction. It took all of Grace's self-control not to groan.

"So that's the new vicar. Mr. Pollack, the squire's coachman, came to see Mr. Gray late yesterday and mentioned that the vicar had arrived. Being a man, of course, he neglected to give my husband all the juiciest details like how very handsome a man Mr. Havenhurst is. But then, I'm not telling you anything you haven't already noticed, am I, Miss Edgewood?"

"I suppose he is well enough. Ah good, I see your husband returning with my horse. I'll say good-bye. Thank you for your hospitality, Mrs. Gray."

And Grace fled.

It was the slowest week Grace had ever survived. Looking at her reflection in the mirror that Sunday morning, she couldn't help but notice how pale her cheeks

were and the dark smudges under her eyes. What a low-
ering turn of events, having to admit to herself that the
advent of a mere man into the parish could upset her
self-possession to such a degree that it showed physically. It wasn't as if she had set eyes on him since
Wednesday anyway!

But finally Sunday had arrived, and she could see him
again. Her fine eyes rolled at the silly, schoolgirl thought,
but she couldn't deny the rush of butterflies that took
flight in her breast.

What in heaven's name was the matter with her? It
wasn't as if she hadn't had many beaux before—real
beaux who had courted her properly, even if it was only
for the short time before her brothers succeeded in fright-
ening them away. But this new vicar had invaded her
thoughts in a way none of the others had, not even Wil-
liam Drake, the boy who had managed to persist in his
suit long enough to declare himself to her before turning
tail and running.

No, Grace had to admit that this one was different,
and not just because, for the first time in her twenty-four
years, she was far enough away from her brothers that
they could not intimidate her suitor. There was something
about the Honorable Adam Havenhurst that touched
her—all of her!

What she didn't quite know was what to do about it.
She couldn't throw herself at a vicar! She would just
have to hope that fate brought them together often
enough, and in such a manner, that he would be able to
see her in the same favorable light.

"Grace, are you going to stand there gawking at yourself in the glass all day, or are you going to attend services with us? The girls are coming down the stairs now."

"I'll be down in a moment, Mrs. Stiles!"

Grace frowned at her image. Mrs. Stiles, she had said
formally, just like she always did when she thought their

students might be within earshot. The title was a misnomer, of course. The only Mr. Stiles that Grace had ever met was Margaret's brother. There had never been a husband to bestow the title on Margaret; only age and courtesy had done that.

She glanced back at her image and shook her head. When would she become Mrs. Edgewood instead of miss? Was there a magic age when one did that?

Grace walked slowly to the top of the stairs, her gaze falling on the students assembled in the hall below. A week ago, she had found her position at Dodwell Academy all she needed, all she desired.

"Hurry, Mith Edgewood!" lisped Polly, one of their youngest students.

Grace started, shaken out of her reverie. Polly's pronunciation had sounded too much like "Mrs. Edgewood" for comfort. Shivering, Grace forced a smile to her lips and descended the stairs.

"I wouldn't want to miss any of the new vicar's sermon," said her uncle, offering her his arm to descend to their carriage.

"Nor would I," she concurred, her own thoughts and expectations very different from her dear uncle's.

"Where is my cravat, Mrs. Odstock?" called Adam, poking his head out of his bedroom and waiting impatiently for the grumbling figure of his housekeeper to appear.

"It's here, Mr. Havenhurst, it's here, and good as new. You really should have some homespun clothes made up if you're going t' be working like a farmer about the place. I can't mend everything!"

The cravat she thrust into his hands was snowy white except for one ragged row of ecru stitching. Adam couldn't prevent that supercilious brow from rising as he gazed at it in dismay. Immediately, he schooled his features to a brittle smile, but the old crone was not fooled.

"I know it's not what you're used to, Vicar, but you've only yourself to blame. Fancy forgetting to pack your cravats," she said, "and not a proper tool in the house— no white thread, no fine needle. What's more, I warned you I'm no lady of the manor; when I stitch up a rip, it's done with service in mind."

"Thank you, Mrs. Odstock. I appreciate your efforts, and I'm sure I'll be able to tie it in a fashion that will hide the tear."

With a grunt, she nodded, saying, "If that's all, I'm wantin' to get over to the church. The entire village will be there for your first service, you can be sure of that."

With a cackling laugh, the old woman made her way down the stairs and out the front door, leaving Adam to wonder which would please his housekeeper more—if his first efforts in the pulpit were a rousing success or a bitter failure. Fortunately, he reflected, most of the parishioners he had met had been nothing like the acerbic Mrs. Odstock.

After several failures which left the fine fabric limp and lifeless, Adam decided to settle for a rather lopsided Oriental. There had been a time when he would have refused to leave his house after such a disaster; now, he found he hardly cared at all. The only ones who might notice were the squire's son, visiting from university, and other callow youths. As vicar, he took no notice of them, he told his image before tucking the ragged stitching inside his coat collar once again.

The sun, shining through the trees, dappled the ground with light as he crossed the road and strolled the hundred yards to Pixley Chapel, as the local people called the church. It was a lovely building of gray stone, perhaps four hundred years old, with a modest steeple that held a rusted bell that hadn't worked, the locals said, in the past century. Inside, the walls had recently been white-washed and the wooden pews polished until they gleamed. The stained-glass windows, rumored to have been stolen from a French church, were the pride of the village.

Adam glanced through his notes one last time before entering through the side door and into the pulpit. He reminded himself that he had been a clergyman for five years, and though he had never been a village vicar, he certainly had enough experience to be calm about this first effort.

He ignored the clanking of his knees as they beat together. He ignored the way his hand shook as he placed his notes on the lectern; he even caught them in midair when a sudden draft sent them fluttering toward the cold stone floor, and then smoothed them while staring across the sea of expectant faces.

"Good morn—ing." His voice broke like a schoolboy's. He gazed at that relentless sea of faces, and the capacity for rational thought and speech fled.

Then he spied her, a bright shining beacon in that treacherous sea, and his mind cleared, his speech returned. Even as he gave the best sermon of his life, he marveled at her bewitching hair and eyes, her full lips, and her heavenly curves. Miss Edgewood was the most perfect female he had ever met, and he had met many during his years on the Town in London, before making his decision to join the clergy.

Finally, the service was ended, and he stood by the door, greeting his parishioners one by one, from the youngest to the oldest. He accepted an invitation from the squire and his wife to join them for dinner. He promised to call on Mrs. Applegate, whose sister had related every detail of her latest misery. All the while, he kept watch for Miss Edgewood, but she never appeared, and he decided she must have slipped out the side door.

Mrs. Odstock shook his hand and gave that strange cackle again. This time it was accompanied by a smile, so he judged that his sermon had pleased her.

"I'll be dining with the Lamberts, Mrs. Odstock, so you may have the entire day off," he said quietly.

"The Lamberts, eh?" she said, her eyes narrowing as she leaned closer and whispered, "Watch yourself, Vicar."

"Watch? I'm afraid I don't . . ."

But the next villager was already placing his hand in Adam's, and he was forced to turn his attention away from the cryptic Mrs. Odstock.

All thoughts of the odd old woman fled when he looked up to find Miss Edgewood holding out her gloved hand for him to shake. Without considering his audience, Adam bowed over her hand, brushing the back of it with his lips. Her eyes were alight with pleasure when he straightened to gaze into her face.

Grace had been watching him intently throughout his sermon, watching the raggedly stitched tear creep out of his collar and watching him tuck it back in. It was out again, and without considering her audience, she tucked it in for him, allowing her hand to rest on his neck for only a half of a second before realizing how her gesture would be taken and jerking her hand away, her clear complexion flooding with color. With a muttered farewell, she darted away, leaving him to deal with the next parishioner.

"I am Rhodes Dodwell, Mr. Havenhurst."

"How do you do?" he asked, relieved to lose himself in the simple courtesy. "I don't believe we've met, have we?"

"No, I am Grace's uncle. And this is another of our teachers, Mrs. Stiles."

"I'm very happy to meet you, Mrs. Stiles. Your students are very well behaved, even the youngest ones."

"Thank you, Mr. Havenhurst. We are very proud of our little school. You should come and visit us soon. I would love to discuss our Latin and Greek curriculum with you. I sometimes wonder if we are challenging our students enough," said the older woman.

"Latin and Greek? I thought your pupils were all girls," said Adam.

"Why, yes, but there is no reason they cannot learn the language of Plato, too. But I have taken enough of your time," she said, glancing behind her where several more people were awaiting their turns with the new vicar. "Please do stop by for a visit."

"Thank you, Mrs. Stiles. I look forward to it."

He followed her progress to her carriage, hoping to catch a glimpse of Miss Edgewood. He was not disappointed, although she jerked her head back when she realized he was looking at her. His lips twitched in amusement as he turned back to the next person in line.

Finally, Adam was able to close the church doors and trundle home. He was feeling quite self-satisfied, and not a little bit relieved to have this first public effort over with. Humming the little ditty he had heard Miss Edgewood sing to her students, he made his way back to the tiny vicarage.

"That Miss Edgewood made quite a spectacle of herself, didn't she?"

Adam jumped at the sound of his housekeeper's voice.

"What are you doing here, Mrs. Odstock? I gave you the day off," he said, following her into the kitchen and sitting down at the table.

"And so you did, but I knew you'd be needing something to sustain you before making your way to the squire's table. That wife of his never could set a decent table, to my way of thinking. Not that I've ever been invited, of course, but that's neither here nor there. I've heard about it, and I couldn't allow you to spend your day living on expectations and being sorely disappointed."

"That's very kind of you, Mrs. Odstock, but I could have found something to eat."

"Nonsense, that's what I'm here for, Vicar. Besides, I wanted to warn you before you set out this afternoon."

"Warn me? You said something to that effect before. What do you mean?"

"Just this," she said, sitting down opposite him without being invited, something a proper housekeeper would never do. "The squire's wife has more than dinner in mind." She punctuated this puzzling statement with a wink.

"And what might that be?" said Adam.

"There's a Miss Lambert, don't you see. A Miss Lambert who had been sent to Bath for a little town polish until you arrived in Pixley. Now, she's back home again, all of a sudden like, and I'll leave it to you to draw your own conclusions."

His raised brows and blank look provoked her to snap, "She's looking for a husband, and that mother of hers thinks you're the most likely candidate."

Adam laughed and shook his head. "I appreciate the warning, Mrs. Odstock, but I assure you, before I became a mere vicar, I was hunted by the most experienced mamas in London, and managed to slip their knots. I think I can handle Mrs. Lambert."

"Humph! Judging from the spectacle you allowed that Miss Edgewood to make of you this morning, I take leave to doubt that!"

"She was only tucking in the torn bit of my cravat. It was a mere kindness—a reflex, nothing more."

"In another young lady, perhaps, but Miss Edgewood is not just any young lady."

Adam's brown eyes turned black, and his nostrils flared as he looked down his nose at her. He would not tolerate intolerance in his own household. "And what do you mean by that?"

The old crone stood her ground. "I mean, Mr. Havenhurst, that any female who has a special house for bathing built, who teaches young girls to flaunt themselves . . . well, young lady is not a term I would use to describe her. But I'm too much of a lady myself to say the term you should use!"

Before he could question her further, she threw her shawl around her shoulders and stalked out the back door.

"What the de—" Frowning fiercely into his teacup, the Honorable Adam Havenhurst was torn between his duty and his desires. He sighed, wishing for the hundredth time that his chosen profession came easier to him.

But what could he expect? He had chosen to become a clergyman as a sort of penance for his misspent youth. As the younger son of an earl, he could have purchased a commission in the army. That's what several of his friends had done after the debacle that had left a young woman dead. Adam shuddered, wondering anew what could have possessed that girl's father to commit murder over her failed elopement with one of his friends.

The experience had ruined them all, aging them in a way that years could not. So the groups of friends had dissolved, the majority joining the army. But for Adam, this had seemed like the cowardly course to choose, especially since the war with Napoleon was coming to a close. So he had chosen the Church.

One thing was certain, Adam reflected with another sigh, his choice had proven more of a challenge than he had ever thought possible. The struggle a soldier faced— man against man, was nothing compared to the struggle of a self-centered clergyman—man against himself.

Even now, as he tried to pray about this ongoing dilemma, the bewitching image of Miss Edgewood crept into his mind's eye, distracting him from the more important issues of life.

Giving in to this image, Adam decided that Mrs. Odstock's opinion was colored by her own sour disposition. He simply couldn't believe that the heavenly Miss Edgewood was involved in anything so very wicked.

But she and the other occupants of that school were members of his flock, and Adam determined to visit Miss Edgewood's school the very next day—just to set his mind to rest. It was his duty as the new vicar, after all, to tend to all the members of his parish.

The mere thought of seeing the divine Miss Edgewood again erased the frown from Adam's brow, replacing it with a faraway smile. A longing such as he hadn't felt in a long time came over him, and he groaned.

Temptation, it seemed, could come in all forms. He just hadn't met anyone in a long time who could awaken those baser desires. Miss Edgewood was hardly the fiend Mrs. Odstock hinted at, but she was definitely a temptation.

Smiling again, Adam decided he might find a great deal of pleasure in fighting this particular temptation.

Three

"I'm afraid I have the headache," said Grace, laying her hand on her brow dramatically. She refused to admit, even to herself, that her reason for avoiding the outing was cowardice. She had felt such a fool after touching the vicar's cravat like that. What had she been thinking? Rather, as usual, she had acted without thinking and now would have to pay the price.

"Then you'll just have to get over it, my dear. We have accepted Mrs. Lambert's invitation to dinner, impromptu though it may have been, and we cannot disappoint her or our girls," said her uncle, holding out his hand to help her rise. "You'll see; you'll have a wonderful time once we arrive."

"I don't see how," said Grace, her voice sounding petulant even to her own ears. "You, Uncle, will closet yourself with the squire over the backgammon board, Margaret will play the pianoforte while the other matrons doze, and I will be left to chaperon the girls while fighting off the advances of that spotted coxcomb, Richard Lambert."

"With Pamela and the other girls there, surely he will have other fish to fry," said her uncle, leading her toward the front doors and the huge traveling carriage where Mrs. Stiles waited with their three oldest students, all bosom friends of Millie Lambert, home for a visit from Bath.

"Besides," said her doting uncle, "you are looking so pretty tonight. I should think you'd want to show yourself off a little."

"And you, Uncle, are a conniving rogue . . . but thank you. You have made me feel better."

Resigned to a long evening, Grace pasted a smile on her face as she entered the carriage. She wished for the hundredth time that she had learned to play the pianoforte well enough that she could be the one escaping to its relative obscurity after dinner. But being the only daughter in a household with four older brothers, her practice sessions on this instrument had invariably been interrupted by one brother or the other making up silly lyrics to the piece she was attempting and singing at the top of his lungs until she had fallen off the stool, laughing. Worse yet, they would walk through the room, their hands over their ears, and howl like dogs. Neither behavior had encouraged her in her musical studies, and since she also possessed only a passable voice, she was doomed to be the young lady without any talents at every social gathering.

"If you are really unwell, Miss Edgewood, we can all send our regrets," said Pamela Baxter, a young lady of true nobility and sensitivity.

Her concern made Grace shake her head. "I will be fine, I assure you. I'm certain Mrs. Lambert's excellent dinner will soothe my megrims." She smiled at the three girls in the rear-facing seat and said, "You must be excited about seeing Millie again. I daresay she will have all sorts of tales to tell about her stay in Bath."

"I can't wait to see her! Millie wrote and told us she has cut off all her hair," said Diana Cochran, a vibrant little brunette whose long hair was her pride and joy.

"Remember, we must call her Millicent now that she is 'out,' " said Olivia with a toss of her red curls.

"Olivia, do try to recall that it is because of Millicent Lambert that you are invited to dinner this evening, as well as to the ball that is being given to welcome the new vicar," said Mrs. Stiles.

"The new vicar," said Olivia, who noticed everything about the males she met. "Isn't he the handsomest man you have ever seen? I wager that his robes cost more than all the old vicar's worldly goods."

"Olivia Wood! That is blasphemy!" Pamela gasped.

"No it isn't! He's just a man!" snapped Olivia, her green eyes flashing.

"Girls! I forbid you to speak about the vicar like that. And, Olivia Wood, young *ladies* do not place wagers," said Mrs. Stiles.

"Still," said Diana, "if the robes were so elegant, can you imagine what his coats are like?"

"Now, that's quite enough of that," said Mrs. Stiles.

In the silence that followed, a distracted Miss Edgewood murmured, "By Weston, I should think."

The occupants of the carriage were shortly to have the opportunity to judge the new vicar's coat for themselves. After the formal curtsies and greetings, the three girls took their old friend to one side and did just that. As for Mrs. Stiles, though she might publicly decry her students' comments on the new vicar's dress, she studied it nonetheless, and decided their new vicar was indeed a man of taste and means. His coat and waistcoat were a severe black; even his pantaloons were black, a fact she noted with a growing blush.

With an impudent grin, Grace nodded toward the vicar and whispered, "You see. It has to be Weston. I well remember my brother James coming home with a coat by the great man. He wouldn't take it off for weeks."

"Grace, really, you shouldn't encourage the girls. It is

improper for young ladies to speak of, much less to notice, such things. As for you, you are an unmarried lady, too, and such matters should be beyond your notice."

"You, too, are unwed, *Mrs.* Stiles, but I noticed you studying the new vicar."

"Only his coat," lied the old spinster, turning a deep red.

Grace immediately put her arm around her friend and begged her pardon. It was unforgivable to mention the fact that the older woman's use of the title "Mrs." was only a courtesy.

"You know I did not mean to allow my tongue to run away like that, dear Margaret. Please forgive me."

"Of course I forgive you. As if I could do otherwise—you who have been so kind to me."

"Now, now, let's have none of that, Margaret Stiles. You know very well who is the real backbone of our school. Without you, there would be no Dodwell's Progressive Academy for Young Ladies."

Mollified by this admission, which was nothing but the truth, Mrs. Stiles smiled again and patted Grace's hand.

"There, there, I know you can't help it, not that what you said is not the truth. But when a woman gets to be my age . . . Still and all, I am happy with my life," she said, her eyes straying toward Grace's uncle for only a moment before she returned her attention to the small gathering.

Richard Lambert and his pretty sister Millicent were in the middle of a group of chattering young people. Mrs. Brough, the dressmaker, was also present, chatting with Mrs. Lambert, who was her sister. Lord and Lady Briscoe arrived with the Wilkens family, and the party was complete. The Lamberts' butler announced dinner, and they left the comfortable drawing room behind for the more formal elegance of the dining room. Mrs. Lambert might be the wife of a country squire, but she prided herself on her dinners—even though her cook's efforts were less than stellar. As their hostess was fond of telling her husband, it was the Society that gathered at her dining table that was important, just like at Almack's. This evening, there was an indifferent roasted leg of lamb with stewed yams and green peas, followed by the second course, featuring a passable braised ham with a remove of custard, and a dry fillet of sole with a remove of apple tart.

This evening, Grace found the food remarkably flavorless. Seated across from Millicent Lambert, who had her brother's friend on one side and the handsome Mr. Havenhurst on the other, Grace had no appetite. Whatever attraction they might have felt for each other, she had to admit that Mr. Havenhurst was unaware of it—and of her. Grace rarely looked up from her plate for fear of seeing him smiling down at the insipid girl by his side; whenever she did, it was to witness some inane exchange that made her stomach perform a strange plummeting motion. It was quite apparent that the new vicar had forgotten all about her.

"When I visited Bath as a child because of a lingering cough, I found the water absolutely vile," said Adam, glancing at his dinner companion before returning his gaze to Miss Edgewood. Would she never look up at him? He would not have guessed that she would act so shy and gauche at table. Foolish, of course, but in his imagination he had assigned all sorts of virtues to the beautiful Miss Edgewood, including the very best social graces.

"I never actually tasted it," confided the pretty Miss Lambert with a giggle. "One sniff, and I pushed it away, vowing I would never let anything with such a horrid odor pass my lips."

"Tell me, Miss Lambert, will you be going to London

for the Season next spring?" demanded the youth on her left.

"Mama has promised that I might, if I don't settle on a suitable match before then," said the young lady, turning and gazing soulfully at the new vicar, who had difficulty in refraining from spewing his wine across the table.

Coughing to disguise the choking sound, Adam turned his attention to his other dinner partner, the hostess, who was determined to speak only to Mr. Wilkens on her left, leaving Mr. Havenhurst no choice but to speak to her unmarried daughter.

His coughing caused Grace to look up, finally, and when she met his gaze, he winked at her. Grace blinked. Surely she had imagined that intimate action. But no, there it was again, followed by an impish grin. Her heart did a somersault, and she smiled in return.

"Miss Edgewood, I do hope you'll help me watch over these young people on Thursday night."

Grace turned reluctantly to her hostess and nodded. There was no mistaking the hard glance of a grasping mama protecting her young. Nothing else would have triggered such a lapse of good manners, causing Mrs. Lambert to lean forward and speak out of turn to someone who was not her assigned dinner partner.

"Of course I will, Mrs. Lambert."

"I knew I could count on you, my dear. So mature and levelheaded," said the older woman with a sly smile. With this she resumed her conversation with Mr. Wilkens, a sure signal to the vicar that he must return his attention to her daughter who was seated on his other side.

As for Grace, she obediently returned her attention to her plate.

* * *

After dinner, it was as Grace had predicted, with the exception that Richard Lambert appeared to have forgotten his infatuation with her in favor of Pamela Baxter's blue eyes. Breathing a sigh of relief for this small favor, Grace settled into a chair to listen to Mrs. Stiles's expert performance on the pianoforte. The gentlemen spent little time over their port and cigars, led by the younger set to join the ladies as quickly as possible. Grace watched as Millicent Lambert snared the new vicar's attention before anyone else could. Her uncle and the squire settled in the corner at a small table with the backgammon board already set up for them. Mr. Wilkens and Lord Briscoe were discussing fertilizer while their wives sat side by side on a gold-striped sofa, dozing peacefully.

The vicar appeared quite content to remain in Millie's pocket all evening. If he smiled at her one more time, Grace thought her teeth would surely break, she was gritting them so.

Mrs. Lambert and her sister, Mrs. Brough, were having a comfortable coze by the fire, ignoring the rest of the guests and leaving the role of chaperon to Grace.

Not that there was a great deal to do. They were a well-behaved group of young people; even Olivia, who loved to flirt and did it so well, was splitting her attention between the Wilkens boy and Christopher Sand, another of Richard Lambert's school chums.

Thoroughly bored, Grace lost herself in a daydream where she had only three or four children gathered around her. Wisely, she didn't question why they all had copper hair and dark brown eyes.

Nearby, Adam listened with half an ear to Millicent Lambert's heavy-handed attempts at light conversation. He glanced at Grace from time to time, hoping for rescue, just as he had that first day they had met. Again, she seemed determined to ignore him.

Glancing up every now and then, Grace watched the vicar smile and nod while Millie cooed about how fascinating his occupation must be. She grinned as his eyes rolled in his head, and he glanced around the room, obviously searching for some means of escape.

Suddenly, Adam excused himself and broke away from Miss Lambert. As he approached Grace, her pulse began to race, but his opening gambit set her straight immediately. He was playing his role as spiritual adviser, not attempting to have a polite conversation with her.

"I don't know if you've noticed, but the young people keep slipping out the doors—to the garden, I presume—on the pretext of getting a breath of fresh air," he said in a low voice.

"It is a bit stuffy in here," said Grace, attempting to mask her disappointment as boredom over this commonplace conversation.

"Yes, but if you look around, we are the only people left in the room who are . . . well, somewhat young. I know the girls are in your charge, Miss Edgewood, and I thought you would be interested. Forgive me if I have bothered you." Looking down his aristocratic nose at her, he turned away.

Grace rose and glanced around the room, realizing that what he said was true. Except for Pamela and Richard Lambert, who were sitting much too close in one dark corner, the rest of the young people had vanished, even Millie.

"Pamela," she said, causing the young couple to spring apart, "may I speak to you for a moment?"

The girl hurried to her side, her face a beet red. Richard Lambert followed more slowly.

"We were wondering if you two might help us find the others. They appear to have gone for a stroll, and we don't want them to forget the time." said Adam, striving for a diplomatic tone.

"Or to forget themselves," came Grace's mordant comment.

She linked arms with her pupil and headed for the doors that led to the terrace. As they opened the door, a feminine squeal rent the air. Mrs. Stiles's hands slipped on the pianoforte, causing a jarring crash in the flowing melody. Mrs. Lambert and Mrs. Wilkens pushed past Grace and stepped onto the terrace.

"Millicent! What is the meaning of this?" demanded Mrs. Lambert. Without waiting for her reply, she rounded on Grace, saying, "Is this your idea of chaperoning your students?"

"We were only playing Blind Man's Bluff," wailed Millicent Lambert, removing her shawl from Christopher Sands's eyes.

"I am certain you were, my dear girl, but this is neither the time nor place for children's games. If Miss Edgewood had been doing her job . . ."

"Forgive me, Mrs. Lambert," said Adam, stepping between Grace and the matron, "but it was my understanding that Miss Lambert was out of the schoolroom. Surely, as her mother, it is your job to chaperon your daughter?"

Mrs. Lambert's lips pursed, and she turned on her heel, grabbing her daughter's hand and dragging her back into the drawing room. Seeing all eyes watching them, she said in a tight little voice, "Such silly young people, playing a children's game at a dinner party. Ah, well, one must forgive youth its little peccadilloes, *n'est-ce pas?*"

Grace walked over to the pianoforte and said quietly, "I think we should be going, Margaret."

"But the tea tray hasn't even been brought in," protested her friend.

"To leave now, Miss Edgewood, would surely appear to be an admission of guilt," said Adam, who had followed her. Keeping his voice soft, he said, "Besides, I would hate to be deprived of your delightful company so early."

"You mean that the evening would be over if all of us leave, and then your time with Miss Lambert would perforce be cut short. What I don't understand, Mr. Havenhurst, is how you came to let her out of your sight long enough to think up such an exploit."

"Grace." Margaret Stiles gasped.

"I beg your pardon, Miss Edgewood, Mrs. Stiles, for intruding. Now I understand the meaning of the expression 'shooting the messenger.' " With a sketchy bow, he crossed the room and found his host, determined to spend the rest of the evening as far as possible from all the females present.

"I still say you owe Mr. Havenhurst an apology," said Margaret before closing the door to Grace's bedchamber and leaving her for the night.

Grace blew out the candles by her bed and plopped down, her arms crossed and her eyes flashing fire.

"Apologize to that priggish man? I think not!"

Resolutely, she crawled into bed, determined to sleep. An hour later, her determination had slipped, and she finally admitted that she was much too upset to sleep.

There was only one thing to do. Rising, she removed her night rail and donned her woolen bathing costume. Grabbing a large towel, she began the long trek down the back stairs and through the enclosed corridor to the bathhouse. A vigorous swim was the only thing that would relax her enough to let her find sleep.

Lighting the fires that the servants kept ready was no easy task. The bathhouse, with its huge pool and thick stone walls, was difficult to heat, but by the time Grace finished lighting both fires, she was ready to plunge into the cold waters.

In the moonlit night, another sleepless inhabitant of Pixley was seeking solace in exercise. In London, a midnight ride through the streets had held dangers very different from a ramble through the woods around Pixley. Here, his only fear was coming across a poacher or tripping and falling on his face.

Before he knew it, Adam found himself facing the open gates to Rhodes Dodwell's estate, the sign over the entrance identifying it as Dodwell's Academy. At the end of this long drive, he would find Miss Edgewood. A quick recollection of her caustic tongue made him turn Caesar away—not that he had any idea of knocking on the door and speaking to her, not at this time of night.

Adam stopped. He could see the glow of house lights in the distance. It wouldn't hurt to check out the lay of the land, he thought, entering the gates and riding slowly toward the house.

The light, however, was not coming from the house. It was dark and quiet. The light shone from another building, east of the house. He left the drive to investigate.

So this was the infamous bathhouse. It was quite large, but he had visited other country estates that boasted bathhouses. There was nothing so scandalous about that, and surely there was nothing wrong with girls learning to swim.

Adam cocked his head to one side as he listened to the ditty Miss Edgewood had sung that day when she was teaching her students about the trees. His eyes widened when he realized the words were not about trees, but the appalling innuendos the lightskirts sang.

Corn Rigs and barley rigs
Corn rigs are bonny
I'll ne'er forget that Lammas night
Amang the rigs wi' Annie.

Where the deuce had Miss Edgewood, a gently bred female, learned these words? Shocked and disillusioned, Adam sought an explanation. Perhaps the person singing was Mr. Dodwell. That gentleman had a rather high-pitched voice; perhaps he was the one in the bathhouse. Certainly, it was unusual to think that Miss Edgewood would be swimming at . . . one o'clock in the morning.

Adam gritted his teeth and tried the door, but it was locked. Slowly, he began to scale the walls to the windows set high in the stones. He simply had to know who was singing those words!

"Who's there?" called Grace, pausing midstroke and silently treading water. A chill ran up her spine, and she swam to the edge of the pool, pulling herself out effortlessly.

"I said, who's there?" she called, irritation more than fear infusing her tones. She thought the village boys had finally given up trying to look at the girls through the high windows.

Suddenly it occurred to her that Richard Lambert and his friends might try to do just that. Without thinking of her appearance or her safety, Grace unlatched the heavy door and stepped outside.

"Who's there?" she demanded.

"Whoaaaaaaa!" cried Adam as he lost his footing and began a rapid descent, the stones tearing at his hands.

"Mr. Havenhurst! You! Of all people!"

"So . . . orry, Miss Edgewood. Didn't mean to intrude. I saw the light; I thought someone might be in trouble; I—but you're fine," he said, climbing to his feet and dusting off his breeches. "So good night, Miss Edgewood. Good night."

Backing away, he hurried toward the shadows and obscurity.

Grace stepped into the bathhouse, closed the door, and locked it. Then she began to laugh . . . and laugh . . .

and laugh. Just when she thought she had regained her composure, another fit of the giggles would overtake her until she was weak and giddy.

Hidden safely in the woods, Adam cursed his luck and his own stupidity. One thing was certain, however; Miss Edgewood was not the lady he had thought her to be. No lady would ever sing that song. And a lady wouldn't be swimming in the middle of the night, nor would she go outside and speak to a man. Why, for all she knew, it might have been a brigand, some sort of ruffian planning to ravage her.

Unless, of course, she was expecting someone else—a lover, perhaps.

Even as her peals of laughter burned into his soul, Adam Havenhurst, vicar of the parish of Pixley, saw his duty clearly. Miss Edgewood, and her *progressive* academy, had to go!

The next morning, dressed in his best coat and sporting a brand new cravat from Miss Silverton's shop, Adam made his way to Dodwell's Progressive Academy for Young Ladies. He had been most gratified when the groom brought the letter begging his attendance at the school, indicating that an apology in person was forthcoming. Feeling rather smug, he turned his curricle into the gates at five minutes before eleven, the time set for his appointment. The note, which had not been signed, had arrived at the vicarage at nine o'clock. At least Miss Edgewood had wasted no time in realizing she needed to apologize; first, for her nasty remark at the dinner and then—to his mind, the greater offense—for the singing of that limerick followed by laughing at him, a man of the cloth.

Very much on his dignity, Adam climbed down and handed the curricle over to Patrick, the school's groom.

"Good morning again . . . uh . . ."

"It's Patrick, Mr. Havenhurst," supplied the groom who had introduced himself not two hours earlier when he delivered the letter to the vicarage.

Adam said, "So sorry, Patrick. My lamentable memory with names, I'm afraid. I don't know how long I shall be. Perhaps you could take him around to the stables."

"Very good, sir," said Patrick, climbing into the curricle and driving off.

Adam took the opportunity to look about himself. Noting the excellent grounds around the house, it occurred to him that Mr. Dodwell must be a very wealthy man—quite eccentric, too, from what he had observed. He wondered if he would be able to influence such a man, to persuade him to reform his school and his niece, too.

Adam stiffened his resolution and lifted the knocker on the massive wooden door, bringing it down decisively.

"Good morning, Mr. Havenhurst," said the gray-haired housekeeper who answered the door.

Adam knew he had met the woman the day before, after services. He could recall their brief conversation, word for word, but he had no idea what her name was. Handing her his hat, he said, "Good morning, Mrs. uh . . . I'm sorry, I don't recall your name."

"Green, bless you, Vicar, but you don't have to apologize. You've got more important things to do than to remember a poor housekeeper's name," she said, beaming up at him. "But come in, come in. You'll have to excuse us this morning. It is Monday, you know, and we're at sixes and sevens around here. I'll get Mr. Dodwell for you."

"I have an appointment with Miss Edgewood."

"Have you? Well, I will see if I can find her. Would you mind waiting in the library? Second door on the right," Mrs. Green called as she hurried away.

Adam entered the room she had indicated, half expecting to find Miss Edgewood waiting for him. After all, wasn't that what one did when one made an appointment? The library was empty, however, and he began to pass the time perusing the bookshelves. His eyes widened in surprise. Beside the classics of Plato and Ovid were more exotic titles, some he had heard about, but never read. Just as he reached for one volume, the door opened and in walked Mr. Dodwell, his eyes twinkling as he took in the tableau.

Red-faced, like a schoolboy caught in some prank, Adam thrust the book back into its slot before turning to face the older man.

"Good morning, Mr. Havenhurst. So good of you to call. I see you have made yourself at home," said Rhodes Dodwell, crossing the room and removing the book. Leafing through it, he allowed it to fall open to an illustration of two people intwined in a manner which caused Adam—a man of the world—to blush.

"From India. I picked it up in my travels. Can't read a word of it, of course, but all the same, it is quite, ah, informative."

A head taller than Mr. Dodwell, Adam raised his brows and pursed his lips, looking down his nose at the man. "Not precisely what one would expect to find in a school library."

"Certainly not," said Mr. Dodwell, replacing the book and indicating the leather chairs that flanked the wide fireplace. When they were seated, he continued, "But since this is my library and off-limits to our students, I do not scruple to include such rare editions. I am a man of the world, Mr. Havenhurst. I never pretend to be anything else."

"Yet you run a school for young ladies."

"Please do not let my niece hear you say so. No, no, I only supply the funds and the house. My niece and

Mrs. Stiles run the school and look after the girls in our care. I'm just the dancing master," he added with a self-deprecating chuckle.

"But I'm being a poor host. I'm afraid Mondays are always quite hectic around here as we begin our week. Seems everyone has special projects they are beginning. Grace, for instance, is leading her girls out to collect fall leaves. She does so enjoy the study of botany."

"Botany. An unusual course of study for young ladies," said Adam.

"Yes, I suppose, but it has come in handy. You noticed, perhaps, the lovely shrubs and flowers around the front of the house. The girls take care of all that. We have men in from the village to do the heavy work, of course, but my niece and the girls plan it and keep it going."

"I never would have guessed," said Adam, recalling the army of gardeners his mother deemed necessary to keep her gardens up to snuff. "But the other subjects, Mr. Dodwell, surely you don't think they are necessary for young ladies."

"I really do not know what young ladies are supposed to study, only what Grace tells me they should study. And Mrs. Stiles, of course; she is the backbone of our little school. We were very fortunate to find her and lure her away from her old position. She is a treasure," said Mr. Dodwell fondly.

"I'm certain she is, sir, but that is not what concerns me."

"Oh? I'm sorry. I thought you wanted to talk about our little school. I know newcomers often look at us askance. Well, I mean, the name says it all, does it not? Progressive Academy for Young Ladies? Makes people nervous when they think someone is tinkering with tradition."

"I suppose so," said Adam. "So tell me about your school."

"There's not much to tell, Mr. Havenhurst. Our girls are quite bright, and I think they enjoy school. Most of them live on the premises, but a few are day students. We try to provide them with a wholesome environment. I mean, Grace is always telling them to go outside and get some fresh air and exercise."

"Ah, yes, exercise. I noticed the bathhouse."

"Yes, that caused quite a scandal at first, but it was all a hum. I don't think anyone gossips about that anymore, at least, not where we hear about it."

"What else do the girls do, Mr. Dodwell?"

"As I said, they swim, go for walks, and ride. We don't keep a large stable, because . . . well, the only man about the place, other than myself, is Patrick. Mrs. Stiles thinks it wise not to tempt impressionable girls with handsome dancing masters or dashing grooms. Patrick is too, shall we say, plain, and I am too old to inspire desire in an impressionable girl's heart," said Rhodes Dodwell with a chuckle.

"Quite," murmured Adam, shifting uneasily in his seat when a loud exchange in the hall outside the library reached his ears. Mr. Dodwell only smiled, pausing in his conversation to listen. The voices penetrated the room quite clearly.

"I will not apologize, Margaret. It is he who owes me an apology."

"But, my dear Grace, men never apologize. With four brothers, you must realize that. So, if you wish to get past this impasse with the new vicar, it must be you who begs his pardon."

"I will speak to him, but I will not beg his anything!"

The door opened with unaccustomed vigor, and Grace stumbled into the room. She was dressed in an old cotton gown, its flowers faded to a dull monotone. Even in this garb, she was vibrant and beautiful.

"Good morning, Miss Edgewood," said the vicar, rising quickly.

"Good morning, Mr. Havenhurst, Uncle." Grace turned and closed the door carefully. "Is there something you wanted, Mr. Havenhurst? I was about to take the girls for a nature walk."

"I think I should leave you two alone," said the older man, quickly vacating the library before Adam could protest.

What was the matter with this household? Did no one follow the rules of decorum? The door closed, leaving him quite alone with Miss Edgewood and feeling distinctly uncomfortable.

Still, he would not back down. He was a vicar, after all, and she was a member of his parish and under his care. Since her uncle obviously lacked a father's sense of protectiveness, it was clearly his duty to show Miss Edgewood the proper path.

Very well, he thought. He would begin by offering her an olive branch. "As a matter of fact, I thought you asked me to call," he said.

"That was Mrs. Stiles, I'm afraid," said Grace.

"I see. Well, that is neither here nor there. I have my own reason for coming. I thought I should beg your pardon for my boorish behavior last night." Aha! That took the wind out of her sails! And now that he was on her good side, perhaps she would listen to him.

But Grace only flashed him a militant glare and moved closer, taking the chair her uncle had just vacated. Adam placed his elbow on the mantel, creating, he hoped, a very paternal picture.

"Very well, I accept your apology, Mr. Havenhurst, though I still do not understand what you were doing outside the bathhouse so very late last night."

And with that facer, she knocked him flat.

He hadn't meant to, but he puffed up like a peacock

and snapped, "That's not what I was apologizing for. I meant my behavior at the Lamberts'."

"That was nothing compared to your spying on me in the bathhouse," said Grace, beginning to smile.

Adam's dark eyes narrowed, and he asked, "And what were you about, Miss Edgewood—bathing so late, singing lewd songs, and then opening the door? Most young ladies would have screamed for help, but you were hardly surprised. Perhaps that is because you weren't surprised. Perhaps you had an assignation." The thought of Miss Edgewood meeting another man was intolerable, causing Adam to gasp for breath like a drowning man.

For her part, Grace lifted her chin, not bothering to deny his ludicrous accusation. "What I do in my own home is none of your concern, Mr. Havenhurst."

"You think not?" he asked, unable to stop himself. "I daresay the parents of your students might take a different view, Miss Edgewood." By now, his face had turned an ugly mottled red.

"How dare you come in here in the guise of offering an apology when all you really want is to throw out threats and innuendos. But I will not bandy words with you. Good day, Mr. Havenhurst."

Grace rose in one fluid movement, facing him down with a haughty stare—the type of stare some women of the *ton* practiced for hours. The expression brooked no argument. With a hasty bow, Adam stormed out of the study, slamming the door behind him.

Seconds later, the door opened, and Grace's uncle strolled back into the room and observed dryly, "I think that young man has taken a fancy to you, puss."

Four

"You will be so good as to notice, girls, that we are heading due west this morning," said Grace, pointing up at the hazy sky. "By the time we turn to go home, it will be after noon. If anyone should get separated, you must retrace your steps, heading away from the sun."

"But what if we get lost this morning, Miss Edgewood," asked Abigail Heart with her usual irritating smirk.

"Abigail, if you are afraid you'll not be able to keep up with us, do, please, feel free to return to school now."

"That settles you, Miss Saucebox," said Olivia, yanking one of Abigail's curls.

"We will all turn around and go back if I hear one more word of wrangling. Do I make myself plain?"

"Yes, Miss Edgewood," came the choral reply.

"You girls should look upon our nature walks not only as an opportunity to learn about the trees and the world, but also as a chance to stretch your legs, to keep yourself fit and healthy. It takes more than a swimming lesson twice a week to keep the roses in your cheeks."

"Earlier, I heard Mrs. Stiles telling Mrs. Rice that you swim almost every night, Miss Edgewood, and sometimes very late," said Abigail, essaying a sweet smile. "And you had a visitor?"

The other girls gasped, turning immediately on the treacherous Abigail in defense of their champion.

Grace maintained her composure, saying, "You should not be eavesdropping, Abigail. I think you should return to the school and go straight to your room. I will attend to you when I return this afternoon."

"I didn't want to go on this stupid nature walk anyway!" snapped Abigail, heading back the way they had just come.

"Should I go with her, miss?" asked sweet-natured Pamela.

Abigail whirled and let fly, "No, Miss Prim and Proper, you shouldn't come with me! Just because you, Diana, and the horrid Olivia get to go to the ball on Thursday, you think you're all grown up! Well, I'm sixteen, and I don't need a nurse leading me around by the nose!"

Grace left the other girls standing with their mouths sagging open while she went after Abigail. She had no idea there were hard feelings over the Lamberts' invitation. Even though Abigail was a difficult child to like, she was not usually so nasty. By the time Grace caught up with her, she was in tears with great rasping sobs shaking her entire body.

"Abigail, stop, please." The girl stopped, but she didn't turn around. "Abigail, why didn't you tell me you were upset about missing the ball?"

"What could you do about it?" she demanded. "Besides which, I'm not that upset. I don't even like Millie Lambert."

The glimmer of a smile crossed Grace's lips, and she nodded. "I can understand that. So tell me why you are so upset, dear."

"Oh, it's that Olivia. She's been talking about it nonstop."

"Teasing you that you aren't going?"

"Well, no, not that exactly," said Abigail, bowing her head and shuffling her feet. "I'm just so sick of hearing about it. I know I'll have my turn; that's what Amanda keeps telling me, but it's so hard to wait."

"Indeed it is. Well, I am glad we have cleared up this misunderstanding. But, Abigail, you mustn't be eavesdropping and carrying tales, you know."

"I know, miss. I'm sorry. I'll apologize to the others, but I don't want to face them right now. I just want to go home."

"Do you want someone to walk with you?"

"No, I'll be fine. I've lived here all my life; I can certainly follow a little trail through the woods." She gave Grace an impulsive hug and then started on her way.

"Oh, and, Abigail, you might want to take your geography book out on the terrace and read that last chapter. I've planned a little surprise over it for tomorrow."

Abigail grinned and waved.

Returning to her other pupils, Grace quickly calmed their curiosity over Abigail's outburst, dismissing it as a fit of nerves. As they progressed deeper into the woods, she pointed out the many varieties of trees growing around them, encouraging them to collect as many different types of leaves as possible.

At noon, they opened the baskets Cook had sent along for their nuncheon and picnicked on the carpet of green grass in a small clearing.

If not for the niggling regret she felt over losing the vicar—not that she had ever had him, Grace labeled her day a great success. The girls were enthusiastic and well behaved. They really seemed to be learning about the trees and other plants. As they headed for home, and she began to sing her childish song about the oaks and birches, all the girls joined in, singing at the top of their lungs.

The song made her recall Mr. Havenhurst's taunt about her singing . . . how had he put it? Lewd songs. Well, it was true she hadn't sung about the trees the night before, but the words were innocuous enough. After all, John and Gilbert had taught her the song after they had gone off to school that first term. They had laughed and laughed over their little sister singing it.

The seed of suspicion began to grow in her breast. Carefully, Grace analyzed the words her brothers had taught her so long ago.

It was upon a Lammas night
When the corn rigs were bonnie,
Beneath the moon's unclouded light
I held awa' to Annie.

The time flew by wi' tentless heed
Til 'tween the late and early,
Wi' small persuasion she agreed
To see me thro' the barley.

Corn rigs and barley rigs
Corn rigs are bonny
I'll ne'er forget that Lammas night
Amang the rigs wi' Annie.

Her cheeks began to burn as the meaning of the verse crystallized. Had she only known, she would never . . . oh, what he must think of her! Well, that didn't require great powers of deduction. He thought she was as vulgar as the song she sang!

The next time she saw Gilbert and John, she would darken their daylights. Wonderful, she thought, with an audible sigh. Now she had switched from bawdy songs to boxing cant. Why couldn't she have had sisters instead of brothers?

"Miss Edgewood, should we make a run for it?" asked Olivia, holding out one hand to catch the raindrops Grace hadn't even noticed in her agitation.

"Oh, yes, let's move along as quickly as possible, girls," said Grace, taking the hand of the youngest girl and picking up her skirt with the other.

The rain that had been threatening all morning pelted down, soaking the group thoroughly before they could reach their destination. Chilled and sodden, Grace sent them up the stairs before ordering the maids to heat water for baths and hot tea.

As she put her hand on the banister to seek her own room, Mrs. Stiles appeared, leading another group of girls toward the music room.

Sending them ahead, the older woman said, "I hope you plan to have a hot bath, too, my dear."

"Indeed I do."

"Was it a successful lesson, my dear?"

"Yes, I fancy the girls learned quite a bit." Looking around to make certain they weren't overheard, Grace added, "I learned quite a bit myself. Did you speak to Abigail when she came home?"

"Why no, I haven't had a chance. What happened?"

Grace frowned. "She did come down for luncheon, didn't she?"

"How could she do that, Grace? She was with you."

Alarmed, Grace didn't answer, but started up the steps, taking two at a time.

"Whatever is the matter, Grace?" called Mrs. Stiles, following more sedately.

The room Abigail shared with her sister and two other girls was empty. Mrs. Stiles arrived, huffing and puffing.

"I sent Abigail back early; she was in quite a state, sniping at me and everyone else. I thought we came to a better understanding, but . . . Oh, Margaret, where can she be?"

"Now, we mustn't panic. You search this floor. I'll go back down and ask Cook and Mrs. Green if they have seen her before we panic. And I'll ask her sister, of course."

"We must hurry, Margaret. This weather is dreadful. I hate to think of her being caught in this downpour."

"Now, now. If Abigail was still angry, she may very well have walked home to her own house. Is her mother in residence?"

"I . . . I'm not certain. Let's just hurry. If she's not in the house, we'll have to mount a search party," said Grace.

With this, the two women split up and began their search. Soon, everyone was looking for the missing girl, but they finally had to acknowledge that Abigail had not returned to the school.

"I'll take Patrick and go to Abigail's house. If she's not there, I'll send him to the village for some men to begin the search while I retrace our path from this morning. This is one time I wish we employed more grooms."

"Grace, do be careful," said Mrs. Stiles, laying a hand on her sleeve.

Grace had changed into her blue riding habit and had thrown a greatcoat over it. Giving her friend an absent-minded kiss on the cheek, she tied her French walking hat over her blond curls.

"You'll ruin that new bonnet, my dear," said Mrs. Stiles.

"At least it will keep the driving rain out of my eyes," said Grace.

"I'm going with you," said her uncle, rolling into the foyer, dressed in buckskins and boots. "I'm not yet in my dotage that I can't ride in the rain."

"Very well, Uncle. You and Patrick can go to Mrs. Heart's house while I begin my search. You know the area where the girls and I were walking this morning. If you discover Abigail has gone home, you can send Patrick there after me."

Grim-faced, they left the house, bending their heads against the driving rain. It was late September, and the rain had dropped the temperature.

As she rode along, Grace reflected on how glad she was that she had thought to wear the greatcoat that her brother James had left behind when he had outgrown it years before. It had served her well since then; this time allowing her to keep her mind on the search at hand, instead of on her own discomfort.

"Abigail! Abigail!" she called, the wind whipping the words and tearing them to nothingness.

She should have known better than to send the girl back alone, no matter what Abigail said. Knowing how contrary the girl could be, she had probably decided to give everyone a scare and ended by getting herself well and truly lost. If they found her . . . *when* they found her, she would read her a good scold.

Something made Grace turn her horse toward the creek that divided her uncle's estate from the Earl of Foxworth's lands. The water would be rising, turning the tributary into a small river, a dangerous place to be.

At least the rain had slowed, and the wind was dying down, she thought, hunching her shoulders to prevent the cold drizzle from trickling off her hat and inside her greatcoat.

"Abigail! Abigail!"

"Hallooooo!"

Grace whirled her horse around and headed upstream, her heart thumping wildly. Please let it be Abigail!

"Abigail! Where are you?" she called.

"Miss Edgewood? Is that you?"

The voice was obviously masculine, and her heart plummeted.

"We're down here!"

She leapt to the ground and hurried toward the rushing river. The bank was steep and slippery, overgrown with wild vegetation.

"Down here!"

Holding on to a tree, she leaned out, hanging over the rushing river until she spied them.

"Mr. Havenhurst!"

"Glad to know we're still on speaking terms," he said, his smile making her chuckle. "Do you have a rope? I don't think we'll be able to get up to the bank without one."

"No, I don't. However did you happen to fall down at the exact same spot?" Grace demanded, allowing her exasperation to show more than the immense relief she felt.

The vicar shot her a reproving glance and squeezed Abigail's arm. "Well, Miss Abigail slipped and fell, but I came down here on purpose, didn't I, dear?"

Lifting her white face, the miserable, frightened girl nodded.

"We'll talk later, Miss Edgewood. Do you think you could go and find someone with some rope?"

"Certainly! I'm expecting a large search party any moment." She didn't think the exaggeration was too dreadful. With a bright smile, she added, "Don't worry, Abigail. You're safe with Mr. Havenhurst until they arrive. In the meanwhile, I think I'll just ride to meet them."

"Capital idea!" said Adam. "I don't suppose they'll have something to warm us—like brandy."

"I don't know, but here . . ." She removed the wool greatcoat, hooked it on a tree branch, and carefully extended it down to them. "I'll be back soon."

Ignoring the rain, Grace threw herself onto her horse's broad back and turned him toward the house, praying she would not miss the search party. Dusk was closing in; any delay would make the rescue more perilous. Despite her exasperating ways, Abigail was a girl whose health was delicate. If any of the girls sneezed, Abigail contracted a chill. She wouldn't allow herself to consider the consequences of this afternoon's shambles.

Grace wiped the rain from her eyes. They were playing tricks on her; those could not be lights coming her way. Then she shouted for joy as her uncle's old gelding plodded into view.

"I have found them, but we need ropes!" cried Grace, wheeling her horse around to lead the way.

"I've brought ropes and blankets," said Mr. Crane.

"Them?" her uncle asked.

"The vicar is with her. I don't know the whole story, but we will need to pull both of them up. They're clinging to a fallen tree about ten feet from the bank."

"How high is the river?" asked the blacksmith.

"Too far for them to jump, especially with it rushing so. They're just down there," said Grace.

"We'll take the ropes, Miss Edgewood. If you'll open that tarp, I put dry blankets in there."

Grace stayed back while they performed the delicate operation of lifting to safety first Abigail, and then the vicar.

As she placed the blanket around Abigail's shoulders, the girl burst into tears. With the help of the men, Grace mounted and took the girl up behind her. When Adam Havenhurst appeared, Grace reached down and took his hand, squeezing it while her eyes spoke her gratitude.

"She'll be fine. A sprained ankle, I think, but other than that, it was a grand adventure. Right, Abigail?"

Sniffling, the girl nodded and said, "Thank you, Mr. Havenhurst."

"You're very welcome. I'll call on you tomorrow to see how you do. Oh, and, Miss Edgewood, I'm afraid your coat fell into the river. I shall, of course, replace it."

"There's no need for that, Mr. Havenhurst. It was just an old coat. Thank you so much for helping Abigail."

"My pleasure. Here I was thinking country vicars never had any fun." He winked at Abigail and said, "Good evening, ladies."

Adam squeezed Grace's hand once again and then swung up behind one of the farmers on his broad-backed plow horse. With a cheery wave which Grace assumed was meant for Abigail, he rode away. Grace turned her horse to follow her uncle home.

Grace performed the rest of her duties that evening automatically. The doctor pronounced Abigail's ankle a mild sprain. Grace made certain all the girls were settled in their beds before she went to her own room. There, Mrs. Stiles fretted over her while she ate her supper— sitting up in bed and dressed in her warmest nightgown. It had been an arduous day, taxing her mentally as much as physically. While Mrs. Stiles wanted to relive every detail, all Grace could do was remember that lurch of fear that gripped her when she had seen the vicar perched so precariously over that rushing water. His concern had been all for the child, while her concern . . .

Grace closed her eyes. It was so confusing.

"My dear girl, you must forgive me," said Mrs. Stiles, rising and taking the neglected tray off Grace's lap. "Here you are exhausted, and I'm just rattling on. I suppose it comes from being so afraid for you—and for Abigail, too, of course. Now, you just get to sleep, my dear. And you are not to come downstairs at all tomorrow, do you understand? You are to stay in bed all day and . . . sleep or read a book. I insist. Your uncle and I can certainly manage the students for one day. Now, I'll let you rest. Good night, Grace."

"Good night, Margaret, and thank you," said Grace,

turning over in bed and expecting her tumultuous thoughts to make rest impossible.

But when the candle was extinguished, Abigail's description of the vicar's heroic rescue kept playing over and over in her mind. He hadn't been able to get the girl to the bank since she couldn't stand on her hurt ankle, and he hadn't thought to equip himself with a rope when he went out for a ramble. When Abigail had panicked, Mr. Havenhurst had slid down the bank to be with her, assuring her that she would soon be missed, and help would be forthcoming.

The ugliness of their exchange that morning was forgotten as the warmth of her feelings for this man deepened. Yes, Adam—she tried out the name and found it quite comfortable—he might be a little priggish, but his heart was certainly in the right place. At that moment, in Grace's eyes, Adam Havenhurst was a perfect hero, worthy of that role in any of the novels she loved so—despite his predilection for lecturing her. A man of such nobility was surely worthy of her. . . .

No, Grace wasn't ready to admit to such a sentiment, but she couldn't deny the little rush of warmth she felt at the thought of his smile. Hugging her pillow, she shut her eyes and fell asleep, finding contentment in her dreams.

"An interesting day yesterday, Mr. Havenhurst. Make no mistake about that. All the village is talking about it," said Mrs. Odstock.

"Is there anything this village doesn't talk about?" grumbled Adam, dabbing at his dripping nose with his handkerchief.

The housekeeper placed a large pot of boiling water on the table in front of him, threw a towel over his head, and commanded, "Breathe deeply, Vicar. The herbs in there will have you right as rain in no time."

"Humph," came the muffled reply.

"Mr. Gray, the blacksmith, told me that you had slid down that bank on purpose. Miss Silverton—you remember her, the one with the fancy shop—she allows as how you might have a penchant for the younger ladies."

Adam threw the towel aside, glaring at the mustached housekeeper. "Oh, she does? And what do you say, Mrs. Odstock? Is that what you think?"

"No, I think you're more interested in th' schoolmistress than that young school miss. But as I always tell them up in th' village—time will tell."

Adam rose and stalked away. Having grown up a member of the privileged class, he knew the lower orders—from servants to villagers—liked to gossip about their betters, but he had never been privy to their speculations. Mrs. Odstock's frank disclosures made him wonder if he could tolerate living where his actions were under such close scrutiny.

Sitting in the best chair in the tiny parlor, he tried to put aside the housekeeper's conversation and concentrate on his sermon.

Mrs. Odstock appeared before him, her arms crossed as she watched him. She pursed her lips thoughtfully, looking like some sort of mustached fish.

"Was there something else, Mrs. Odstock?" he asked, raising one supercilious brow.

She wiped her hands on her apron and nodded. "You know, Vicar, there's no harm in these folks' observations. If you're to be one of us, you just have to accept the fact that people in Pixley are going to talk about everything and everyone who lives here."

"So you think I should just smile and allow people to shred my character, my reputation."

She expelled that curious cackle that made him want to cover his ears. "Your reputation? Why, if talking about a body was all it took to ruin a reputation, no one in the entire village would have one. Nobody means any harm by it, and you'll do well to remember that, Vicar. If it makes you feel any better, I can tell you all about Miss Silverton and everyone else, too."

Adam held up a hand, shaking his head. "No, that will not be necessary. I wouldn't want to indulge in the same sort of loose talk about my parishioners. Thank you, Mrs. Odstock. That will be all."

"There's one more thing, Vicar. If you don't want to start sneezing all over again, you had best leave the parlor because I have my cleaning to do."

With a sigh, Adam took his pencil and papers and rose. "If anyone should call, I will be over at the church working on my sermon."

"This is Tuesday, Vicar. The ladies will be cleaning the church today. Maybe you should just make yourself scarce. Go for a drive."

"Thank you, Mrs. Odstock. I believe I shall."

Adam made his way to the small barn and hitched Caesar to the curricle. Since there was no peace to be found indoors, he would simply find a quiet spot outdoors. Thankfully, yesterday's rain had moved on, leaving in its wake a crisp, sunny day.

Adam turned the curricle toward the village, not realizing that such an action would mean visiting with every other person who spied him, each wanting to glean any unknown details about the vicar's rescue. Adam kept Mrs. Odstock's counsel in mind and suppressed his impatience, finally stopping and descending at Mrs. Brough's shop.

He and the dressmaker exchanged pleasantries, and Adam again related the story of Abigail's rescue. Then, with an ingenuous smile, Adam broached the topic that had caused him to stop. Mrs. Brough was an excellent businesswoman and managed to hide her surprise at his odd request, taking him into the back room, where she kept a small stock of ready-made items.

Soon, Adam was back in his carriage, a large package on the seat beside him. Waving at Miss Silverton, who had come out of her shop to watch his departure, Adam turned toward Dodwell Academy.

If the direction he took caused speculations, there was nothing he could do about it. He was realizing that as vicar, his parishioners would scrutinize his every action. Fortunately, he thought, he was not just any vicar; being the son of an earl, Adam was arrogant enough to ignore their tittle-tattle.

So, feeling rather pleased with himself, he headed toward the school, which had yet to earn his approval. As vicar, it was his duty to call after Abigail's harrowing escapade. The fact that he hoped to see Miss Edgewood, too, had nothing to do with the tremor of excitement in his stomach when he guided the carriage through the gates and up the long drive. Or so he told himself.

Hopping lightly to the ground, Adam picked up the package and allowed Patrick to take his horse and curricle in hand once again. He soon found himself waiting in Mr. Dodwell's library. This time, he was not tempted to peruse the shelves while he waited for Miss Edgewood to appear, but contented himself with studying his reflection in the small mirror on the mantel, adjusting his cravat and smoothing his copper locks.

After several minutes, the door opened, and Adam turned, his hopes dashed when he saw Abigail making a shy curtsy.

Mrs. Stiles, who was standing behind the girl, gave her a little push. "Go on. Tell Mr. Havenhurst thank you."

"Thank you, Mr. Havenhurst. I'm sorry to have been

so much trouble, and I hope you haven't suffered any . . . uh . . ."

"Permanent injury," whispered the older woman.

"That's it . . . permanent injury."

Adam took the hand she offered and gave it a solemn shake.

"I assure you, Abigail, I suffered no harm at all. I'm glad I happened along to help. Are you feeling better? How is your ankle this morning?"

"My ankle is much improved, thank you, and the rest of me is fine, too."

"I'm glad."

"That was very prettily said, Abigail. Now you may rejoin the others," said Mrs. Stiles. When the girl was gone, she smiled at the vicar and said, "I wanted to thank you personally, Mr. Havenhurst."

"It was nothing. Children will have these little accidents, I am told. And your, uh, friend, Miss Edgewood? Is she about this morning?"

"No, I told her she was not to put so much as a foot on the stairs today. She is confined to her room."

"She is not ill, I hope."

The apprehension revealed in his voice and his dark eyes made Margaret Stiles hasten to reassure him. "No, no, but I think she has earned a day of leisure—as have you, Mr. Havenhurst."

Grinning, he said, "I certainly intended to follow that advice, Mrs. Stiles, if there had been one spot available to me. My housekeeper is very industrious, and the vicarage is very small so I have decided to take my chances with nature once again."

"Poor Mr. Havenhurst. Why do you not simply move into your brother's manor house?" She gasped at her own effrontery. "I beg your pardon, sir. That is none of my business."

"No, no, I'm sure many people in the parish have

asked the same question. Why, I have asked myself the same thing, but the truth is, Mrs. Stiles, a dedicated vicar must do what is best for his parishioners. Living several miles from the church would not be conducive to serving my parishioners."

"I see," she murmured, her tone showing that she didn't really agree with his assessment of the situation.

"And there is also the chance that my brother or mother may decide to visit Pixley. At least in the vicarage, I know I shan't be forced to entertain them!" He grinned and said, "I see I have shocked you. My brother and mother are family, of course, but sometimes they are difficult. You understand, Mrs. Stiles, and I know I can rely on your discretion."

"Certainly, Mr. Havenhurst," said Mrs. Stiles, who was mentally already relating this conversation to Grace, her confidante.

"Good. Well, I mustn't keep you. I really called to see how Abigail and Miss Edgewood fared. Oh, and to give this to Miss Edgewood," he added, picking up the box and handing it to the older woman. He decided it would be best to satisfy her burning curiosity and said, "It's a greatcoat. I purchased it at Mrs. Brough's before coming here."

"I don't understand, Mr. Havenhurst. It is not customary, you know, for an unmarried lady to receive a gift of clothing from a gentleman."

"It is nothing like that. You see, Miss Edgewood gave me her coat yesterday to keep Abigail warm. I'm afraid I let it fall into the river. I only wanted to replace it." He frowned, suddenly concerned that he had overstepped the bounds of polite behavior with his gift. "I certainly don't mean to compromise Miss Edgewood. If you think . . ."

"No, no, I'm sure there is nothing untoward about

such a gift. It is not really a gift at all, is it? It's a . . . replacement."

"Exactly," said Adam, relieved to have the matter settled. The idea of compromising his own position had given him pause, but Mrs. Stiles's sensible viewpoint put the simple gift into perspective.

"I shall give it to her straightaway, Mr. Havenhurst."

"Thank you, and please give Miss Edgewood my best, too. I will take the liberty of calling on her tomorrow, if I may?"

"Certainly, Mr. Havenhurst. We look forward to it. And remember, one of these days, I would really like for you to review my Greek and Latin curriculum."

"I would be delighted. Good day, Mrs. Stiles."

"Good day, sir."

Feeling somewhat deflated, Adam turned to go. His desire to see Miss Edgewood again had been more than a passing fancy. It wasn't merely duty that had brought him to the school, but it was not to be. With a sigh, he walked past the matron and headed toward the front doors.

"Mr. Havenhurst, a moment, please."

A reprieve!

"I hope you won't think me forward for suggesting this, but since you are without a place to work today, I thought you might stay here," said Mrs. Stiles.

"Here? Oh, I wouldn't wish to impose," came the required response.

"It would be no imposition. I don't see why you couldn't use Mr. Dodwell's study. He will be tied up all morning with lessons since he and I are splitting Grace's responsibilities today. I know he would be pleased for you to make use of his little haven."

"I don't know. You really think he would not mind?"

"Not in the least," said Mrs. Stiles. "And I'm certain Grace—Miss Edgewood, I mean—would be pleased to know we had repaid you for the kindness you showed our Abigail yesterday."

"Very well, Mrs. Stiles. I really do appreciate this, and I assure you I shan't take advantage by turning up like a bad penny every day, always in the way. For one thing, I plan to add on to the vicarage as soon as may be."

"Really? The old vicar seemed to think it was quite sufficient, of course, but then he never expected to raise a family there. Being a young man, I suppose you must be thinking of marrying and setting up your nursery."

Adam's brow furrowed. Perhaps he had been too hasty. The last thing he wanted was to feed the fires of gossip about him and Miss Edgewood.

Mrs. Stiles must have guessed his alarm, for she added a blithe, "At the moment, you just need a bit more room for yourself. You're much too young to be thinking of a family yet. When you have been in Pixley a few years, it will be time enough for that."

Adam laughed and breathed a sigh of relief as she left him alone in the study. He set to work immediately, crafting his sermon as a woodworker carves an intricate piece of furniture.

He was deep in thought when a tapping on the window distracted him, and he glanced up to find several pairs of eyes watching him. The girls giggled and waved before skipping back to their "studies" on the lawn—a match of archery. It seemed an unusual course for school, especially for girls, but never having had sisters, he had no way of knowing how unusual. It did seem odd, however, for girls to be studying botany, Greek, Latin, and swimming. He resolved to ask the squire's wife about it. Mrs. Lambert appeared to be a very traditional lady, and she had chosen to send her daughter to Dodwell's Academy; therefore, it couldn't be considered too out of the ordinary.

There was a quiet knock on the door and Mrs. Green, the housekeeper, entered, carrying a tray.

"I thought you might be hungry or thirsty, Vicar."

"Thank you, Mrs. Green. I would like a little something."

"Oh, good," she said, pouring him a cup of tea. "Now, Mr. Dodwell, he sometimes likes to add a bit of something to his tea. He keeps it in the bottom drawer of his desk. Would you like for me to . . . ?"

"No, thank you. I'll just have a little sugar in mine."

"Very good, sir. Oh, and do try some of Cook's little biscuits. They simply melt in your mouth."

"Now, Mrs. Green, you don't want to spoil me so. You'll have me under foot all the time," he teased.

"And that wouldn't be such a bad thing, Mr. Havenhurst. To my way of thinking, we could do with a nice young gentleman around this place." Mrs. Green sat down opposite him and leaned forward confidentially. "Miss Edgewood is such a dear young lady. And a lady she is, you know. Her father was a baron, and now her older brother has the title."

"I take it you have known Miss Edgewood a long time?" he said, despising the weakness that led him to gossip, but unwilling to forego the gratification of learning more about the intriguing Miss Edgewood.

"Oh, my, yes. I was housekeeper to her dear departed mother. When Mr. Dodwell came home and decided to open this school, I knew I had to come, too, to help look after Miss Grace. She's been almost a daughter to me, since her mother passed away almost ten years ago."

"So she was quite young when her mother died."

The housekeeper dabbed a lone tear and nodded. "Fourteen, she was. Just the age when a girl needs her mother. And there she was, saddled with four brothers who did nothing but torment her. Well, you know how boys are with their sisters. Not that they didn't love her."

"Of course," agreed Adam.

"Still, they were such wicked boys. Every time some nice young man showed an interest in Miss Grace, one of them was there to ruin things. No, you mustn't think she's on the shelf for want of suitors; she's had many an offer, but her brothers are a formidable lot. Not a one under six foot tall!"

"Miss Edgewood is quite tall, too," said Adam.

"Yes, and I suppose that did discourage some of the young men. She can be quite formidable, too. But no mistake, she has a heart of gold."

"Who would that be, Mrs. Green?" asked the figure with the heart of gold from the doorsill.

The housekeeper leapt to her feet, dipping a quick curtsy to the vicar before hurrying past her mistress. Grace entered the room, taking the seat her housekeeper had just vacated.

"Please do not be angry with Mrs. Green. I'm afraid I encouraged her," said Adam, unable to tear his eyes away from the vision of Miss Edgewood, who was wearing a plum-colored round gown and looked very much like a schoolgirl herself—a very tall schoolgirl. Golden, springy curls clustered close to her head, and her green eyes, the irises edged in dark blue, returned his gaze without a hint of coyness.

"I daresay she required little encouragement, Mr. Havenhurst, but you must forgive the ramblings of a loyal old servant. I fear she imagines I possess virtues to which only the angels aspire."

"I understand. According to my old nanny, I can probably walk on water. According to my mother, I can part the waters," he added with a self-deprecating chuckle. "I am glad to see you came to no harm yesterday—no chills or ague."

Grace poured a cup of tea and sipped it before replying. "I am much too hardy to let a little rain bring me down. What of you? Are you all right?"

"I came to no harm," he replied.

"Good."

She glanced at the floor, the first sign of maidenly modesty Adam had ever seen her display. He smiled to himself. She leaned over and picked up a biscuit, taking a dainty bite.

"Did Mrs. Stiles give you my little gift?" he asked.

"No, what is it?" she asked, smiling at him.

"Nothing, really, I gave it to her," he said, looking around the room and spying the box on a table by the door. Rising, he brought it back, placing it on her lap.

"I cannot imagine," she said, tearing open the box. "Oh, how thoughtful of you. But really, I cannot accept such a . . ."

"No, no, Mrs. Stiles has already pronounced it quite proper since it is not truly a gift, only a replacement."

"I see," said Grace, grinning at him. "How very clever of Mrs. Stiles."

"I thought so," said Adam with a smile.

She took another sip of her tea, and stared at her cup as if it were positively fascinating.

Conversation lagged until Adam said, "Mrs. Green was right about one thing." She glanced up at him through long lashes. "Your cook's biscuits melt in the mouth."

"Yes, they are my favorite. That is the real reason I decided to come downstairs," she said with an impish grin. "When I received my tea tray, all it had was tea and a rather tired little cake. Then I found out you were here, and I knew Mrs. Green would be plying you with Cook's biscuits—my biscuits—while I was left to starve."

Adam drew back the hand that had been reaching for another biscuit, and he frowned, saying, "I beg your pardon, Miss Edgewood. I had no idea that I was taking food out of your mouth."

Taking the biscuit he had been reaching for, she placed it on the plate in his lap. The intimate gesture made him flush uncomfortably.

Her green eyes wide, Grace appeared oblivious to her indelicacy and continued in the same saucy vein. "Indeed, Mr. Havenhurst, as a vicar, I would have thought you would be more charitable."

Adam placed the plate on the table and stood, saying formally, "I believe I should be going."

"Oh, please do not be so stuffy," said Grace, having the audacity to take his hand and pull him back. The heat of her touch shocked him as much as her words did. "I was only teasing. Are you so starchy that you cannot recognize a joke?"

"On the contrary, Miss Edgewood," returned Adam, knowing he sounded like a hopeless sobersides, but unable to recapture his good humor. "I can recognize a joke, and even expect it when it is delivered by a friend or comrade, but it is unbecoming in a young lady to laugh at the expense of a guest in her own home. Your comments make me realize how very little you understand about the conventions of polite society, and I cannot help but marvel at the number of parents who are willing to place their daughters in your dubious care."

"Why, of all the . . ." Grace leapt to her feet, her eyes narrowing dangerously.

"Please, spare me your abuse. I called to say I am glad that Abigail and you, as members of my parish, came to no harm. But I must also question how such a mishap came to pass. If you wish to keep your school full, may I suggest you take greater care not to lose your pupils."

"How dare you!"

"I dare, Miss Edgewood, because unlike you, I take

my position seriously. Good day to you." As he began to gather his papers, Grace marched to the door and threw it open, her nose in the air. Adam stalked out of the room, grabbing his hat from the table by the front door, and hurrying down the front steps.

"And you can take your coat, too!" yelled Grace, flinging the greatcoat, box and all, at his head, and knocking his hat under Caesar's dancing hooves.

Fire in his eyes, Adam turned and started back up the steps, but Grace picked up her skirts and fled, slamming the front door behind her.

Adam retrieved his tattered hat and placed it on his head. He growled a curse and turned to find an audience of half a dozen girls and Mr. Dodwell. With a curt nod, he climbed into the curricle, picked up his whip, and made good his escape from Dodwell's Progressive Academy for Young Ladies.

Under his breath, he muttered, "It should be called Dodwell's Home for Depraved Lunatics!"

Five

"Oh! That man!" stormed Grace, rushing headlong into the arms of her friend Margaret Stiles.

"My goodness, Grace. What is all this commotion?"

"That man is the most infuriating creature! Do you know what he had the effrontery to say to me?" she said, eyes blazing.

"No, I'm afraid the walls are too thick," said Margaret Stiles, smiling slightly at her own little witticism. When Grace did not smile, she took her by the arm and led her back to the book-filled study. "Do tell me, my dear."

"He said . . . that is . . . oh, never mind," stammered Grace, realizing that she might not come off in a good light if she retold the details of the exchange with the most vexing man in the entire world. Mrs. Stiles would very likely take his side and point out that she had not acted like a very gracious hostess.

"You know, Grace, I do not have a great deal of experience with such matters, but I would say for a man who voices concern over your capability to instruct our students, he seems to spend a great deal of time here. And the fact that you can make the poor man lose his temper in a matter of minutes . . . well, I think that is very telling."

"Telling what?"

"You know. I mean it only goes to show . . ."

"What are you trying to say, Margaret?" asked Grace, frowning again.

"I think your uncle is right. I think Mr. Havenhurst is quite smitten with you."

"Nonsense! The man despises me, and I feel exactly the same about him," she replied, nose in the air.

"Then why did you bother to come down when you discovered he was in the house?"

"Well, I . . . that is . . . I was hungry, and he was eating all of the biscuits."

Margaret Stiles's smirk of disbelief led Grace to toss her head and leave the room. She managed to walk at a dignified pace instead of flouncing out and slamming the door, but she refused to continue such an absurd conversation. It was patent that Mrs. Stiles knew nothing of matters of the heart.

Adam Havenhurst was an arrogant, meddlesome popinjay. She wouldn't even credit him with good intentions . . . trying to warn her that her behavior, her school—why, he might as well have said her *life*—was rubbish! He would no doubt prefer that she left Pixley so he would no longer be troubled with her.

And she, of course, would love to oblige. That way, she would never have to see Adam Havenhurst again!

With this unbearable thought, the usually composed Miss Edgewood burst into tears.

What the deuce was the matter with him? Every time he saw Grace Edgewood, he managed to insult her. And when had he ever been accused of not being able to enjoy a little jest? But no, he had launched into another of his lectures, piling insult on insult.

Adam stopped the curricle and began the task of turning it around in the narrow country lane. He would go back and straighten things out immediately. This time he would truly apologize, humbly and . . .

The jingle of harnesses and the sound of horses' hooves alerted him in the nick of time, and he managed to straighten the curricle just as the traveling coach topped the hill. Barreling down on the small curricle, the driver pulled his team close to the edge of the lane; the coach squealed as the hedgerow scraped along its side.

Adam jumped down while the coach came to a plunging halt. The door of the traveling coach flew open, and the traveler leapt to the ground, hurling curses at the coachman, the country lane, and the air in general.

The tall, dark Corinthian turned his wrath on the country vicar, saying, "You! I might have known!"

Adam stood his ground as the impressive figure approached. He was dressed in the very best London tailors and boot makers could produce, a gentleman of elegance and fashion. His dark hair was styled modishly, but Adam could see that his dark eyes were bloodshot and weary.

"This is a pretty pass, ruining my carriage like this! It will have to be repainted entirely, you know, for the crest is quite ruined on the far side."

"If only you London dandies would realize one can't barrel down a country lane in an overblown carriage like you're racing at Newmarket, it wouldn't have happened," said Adam coolly.

"Right! It's the rough and tumble for you, country bumpkin," said the traveler, putting up his fists. "We'll see if you're as handy with your fives as you are with your mouth."

Adam feinted as the first blow flew. Grinning now, he threw a punch to his opponent's stomach, his fist hitting him squarely. The taller man threw his arms around Adam and held on as they scuffled like schoolboys.

"Eeeeekkkkkk!"

The men sprang apart as the scream tore through the air. Then they set to again, their shoulders shaking as they wrestled.

"Stop them, John! Do something! He's killing my baby!"

"Ma'am, it's nothing like that. Just a friendly little contest."

"Men!" said the matron, hurrying toward the combatants, her parasol raised like a sword. "Stop it, I say! Unhand my son!"

Adam and his challenger turned as one, the taller man's arm still fastened lightly around Adam's neck.

"Are you all right, Alexander? Do you have any idea with whom you are dealing, sirrah?" demanded the diminutive female, striding ever closer.

"Mother, you really must wear those spectacles the physician gave you," said the older man.

"Well, I don't see what that has to do with anything," she said, squinting at the pair. Then her eyes widened, filling with tears. "You will cause me to go to an early grave," she wailed, rushing forward and throwing her arms around Adam's neck, pulling him down to her height with surprising strength.

"Hello, Mother. I had no idea you were coming for a visit. You really should have written to warn me . . . that is, so that I could have been ready for you." Adam detached her arms with difficulty and held her away from him. "You are looking as beautiful as ever, I see."

She smiled at him before turning to the taller of her two sons and rounding on him. "You could have hurt your brother, Alexander. How many times must I tell you that he is not up to your brawling?"

"Mother, I am fine," said Adam, glancing at his older brother over the top of their mother's hat.

Alexander Havenhurst, the Earl of Foxworth, listened

patiently for a moment and then propelled his mother back toward the traveling carriage.

"Yes, yes, Mother, but we must move along; can't keep the horses standing. I'm sure Adam will follow us to the manor, and then you may examine him endlessly to assure yourself that I have not harmed a single pimple on his beautiful face."

"Pimple? Adam doesn't have any spots," she said, dragging her feet as they progressed toward the carriage. "Just follow us, darling," she called over her shoulder.

As the coach pulled away, Adam waved to his mother, whose beckoning hand protruded from the window.

"Damn," he muttered as he climbed back into his curricle, turning Caesar to follow. Moments later, as he passed the gates to Dodwell Academy, Adam wrestled with the overwhelming urge to go through them, feeling somehow he would find consolation in her arms.

In her arms?

The thought, unbidden and forbidden, startled him. A vicar shouldn't be having such lustful fantasies—especially when the object of them was a female whose character he had called into question. Of course, it was not her character he wanted to embrace.

On this alarming note, Adam's grasp of the whip slipped and it touched Caesar's back. Unaccustomed to such a tap, the horse leapt forward, giving the vicar something else to occupy his troubled thoughts for a time.

"Sorry about descending on you like this, old boy, but you know our dear mother," said the earl, signaling the footman, who had brought another bottle of port, to leave them.

When they were alone in the vast dining hall at Foxworth Manor and had sampled the amber liquid, Adam said, "I suppose you held her off as long as you could. Why, it's been almost a week."

Alexander nodded, "Yes, and a very tedious week it has been. I had just installed Christine in my little house on Curzon Street and was planning to become more intimately acquainted, shall we say, when I was summoned home by the usual note."

"Ah yes, the note. Tell me, were there splashes of tears?" asked Adam, his eyes twinkling.

"No, but it was unsteady to the point of being illegible, except, of course, the part demanding that I escort her at once to your side. Seems she had a vision that you were lying on your deathbed."

"Which is why you dropped everything, including your new mistress, and hurried to Pixley."

"Of a certainty, dear brother," said Alexander, his laughter rumbling forth from deep in his broad chest.

"Still, you could have held her off for a little longer, Alex. I mean, if she hadn't yet bothered to weep on the letter, she wasn't totally desperate."

"Well, there were a couple of other reasons why I decided it would be wise to, uh, escape London right now."

"Let me guess, the ladies you have been, shall we say, courting, decided you should settle on one or the other."

There was that laugh again. Alexander took the time to light his cigar before responding, "There was also Colette."

"Colette? I don't believe I know about that one."

"She was the interim mistress before I settled on Christine. She was unhappy with me and threatened to make a scene. A little more money, and she was more complacent about the termination of our short-lived liaison."

"You know, Alex, had the Church never split from Rome, and I were your priest, I don't think I could come up with enough penance for you to perform in order to save your soul."

"I knew I liked old King Henry for some reason."

"A kindred spirit, perhaps, except that he married his ladies," said Adam, peering at his older brother over the rim of his glass.

"And then saw them separated from their heads," said Alexander.

"There is that," said Adam. "There is that." Turning the topic, he asked, "How are my nephews?"

"Very well. Phillip is receiving the highest marks in his class, and my heir has managed to stay out of trouble all term."

"Good for them," said Adam, taking another deep drink. "So, how long do you plan to stay?"

"Mother said something about wintering here in Pixley."

"Egads! You must talk her out of that!"

"Now, Adam, when was the last time I managed to talk our dear mother into, or out of, anything? You are the golden son. You will have to try, but I warn you, it won't be easy."

"It never is. You know, I appreciate her devotion, but I do wish she would see that I am no longer the sickly little lad she nursed and pampered for all those years."

"Impossible. I truly think when she looks at you, she still sees you in short pants and leading strings. Damn, but I'm glad you came along. I quake in my boots at the thought that I might be her only son and subject to all that maternal attentiveness."

"Happy to oblige," came Adam's dry reply.

"So why are you not staying here at the manor? If I remember correctly, I told you to do so. That vicarage is little more than a hovel. Old Henshaw seemed to think he was some sort of religious martyr. Took a vow of poverty or something, and refused to allow me or Father to build him a decent sort of house."

"It's not so bad. The roof doesn't leak over the bed," said Adam. "And I managed to fix the barn door when it fell off. Mind, I had to do so, or I believe Caesar would have bolted. He's accustomed to much better."

"I should say so. And I don't know where you are going to put all the clothes and other knickknacks Mother saw fit to bring for you."

"I saw the trunks; it will never fit at the vicarage," said Adam.

"But you still haven't answered my question, brother. Why not live here?" asked the earl, sweeping a hand about the dark-paneled room with its crystal chandelier and long, polished table.

Adam hesitated. The truth sounded juvenile, even to his own ears. He had told himself and others that his reason for choosing the vicarage over Foxworth Manor was to avoid his mother and brother when they visited. The truth was, for once in his life, he wanted to be truly independent, a man making his own way with the life he had chosen, without his older brother smoothing his path.

Adam met Alexander's penetrating gaze and smiled. Though seven years separated them, they had always shared a remarkable understanding. Spoken words were often extraneous between the two brothers.

Alexander nodded and raised his glass. "To our mother."

"Our mother," said Adam, drinking deeply.

Mrs. Lambert's ball was the talk of the village as well as the favorite topic of the girls at Dodwell Academy. Even Abigail arose from her disappointment at being excluded in order to help the three older girls dress and arrange their hair. As for Mrs. Stiles, she declared Thursday a holiday for the little school, and spent the hours until evening flitting from one chore to another, a bundle of nerves.

For Grace, the day passed in waves of apprehension and excitement. She was delighted with her new gown and looked forward to wearing it. On the other hand, she worried that her next encounter with the vicar would end as all the rest had—in shambles. Still, there was the chance that he might waltz with her, and the rush of excitement this possibility brought was impossible to contain.

The carriage ride to the ball was accomplished quickly, with the girls chattering about the promised treat. When they arrived, the butler ushered them into the drawing room, announcing them in grand style. Mrs. Lambert was on hand to greet them, and the squire hurried forward to welcome them, too.

"Now, Mr. Lambert, you must promise me that you and Mr. Dodwell will not vanish into the card room as soon as dinner is over. This is a ball, and I expect all of the gentlemen to make certain the ladies have partners—especially you, Mr. Dodwell. You are so light on your feet," Mrs. Lambert simpered.

Uncle Rhodes bowed and obediently asked their hostess to grant him the first waltz. The squire's wife blushed like a schoolgirl and accepted. Millie and her brother led the girls away to join the rest of the young people, leaving Grace and Margaret on their own.

In such a small locale, social conventions were not as rigorous, and the guest list included not only the dressmaker Mrs. Brough, who was also the hostess's sister, but the owner of the village's general merchandise store, too. Mr. Crane was the youngest son of a wealthy old lord who had married his housekeeper after his first wife's death. Cast out by his older stepbrothers, Mr.

Crane had managed to take a small annuity and turn it into a thriving business. As a recent widower, Mr. Crane was the target of both Mrs. Brough's and Miss Silverton's matrimonial aspirations. Though Mrs. Lambert would have liked to exclude Miss Silverton in order to give her sister the advantage, the spinster was a distant relation to the Earl of Foxworth and could not be ignored.

Other guests included the families of a retired colonel, two gentleman farmers, one baron, and Lord Briscoe, a viscount who spent most of his time in the gambling hells of London. What Mrs. Lambert had not counted on was the advent into their community of the Earl of Foxworth and the dowager countess. She was in high gig that they had arrived in time for her little soiree and had spent half the day rearranging the place cards at the table, making certain that the earl was on her right and the countess on her husband's right. This, of course, made it difficult for her to engineer her daughter, snaring the new vicar, but after all, the Earl of Foxworth was bigger game.

Grace and Margaret were seated on the sofa facing the door when the butler announced the earl and his mother; the new vicar was relegated to the background in the face of such august personages. It was all Grace could do not to stare at the handsome earl, but his attention was diverted by their hostess, who proceeded to gush and fawn over the new arrivals. Nothing would do but for Mrs. Lambert to lead the earl and dowager countess to her daughter and introduce them, ignoring the other young ladies, her son, and his school chums.

Adam remained in the doorway, watching this performance with a grin. He glanced at Grace, whose twinkling eyes showed him that she, too, appreciated this diversion. He repressed his clerical scruples and winked at her, making her smile—a sight that filled his heart with sunshine.

Heading toward the sofa, he was ambushed by Lord Briscoe, an old acquaintance from his salad days in London. Fobbing him off as quickly as he might, he glanced up to discover that Miss Edgewood had risen and been intercepted by the colonel's wife, whose daughter was a student at their school.

Although Adam hovered nearby, no opportunity presented itself to allow him to speak to her, to apologize humbly to her, for his inelegant behavior two days before.

The butler entered to announce dinner and in the lull, a high-pitched voice rose above all the rest.

"My dear Adam had only to ask, Mrs. Lambert, and he could have had any of several estates. I assure you, he had no reason to become a country vicar *here.*"

"Of course, my dear Lady Foxworth. We feel very privileged to have him here," said the squire's wife, her own nose elevated to meet that of her guest.

"Mother, I believe dinner has been announced. Please do allow me to lead you in," said Adam, crossing the room with feigned casualness.

But Mrs. Lambert, who believed nothing should be left to chance and had carefully orchestrated in her mind how the evening would be played out, beckoned to her husband to lead the countess into dinner. Taking the vicar's arm, she left her daughter to the earl, who offered his escort with reluctance. They fell into line behind Adam.

"Who is that lady in the purple?" his brother asked, bending his head to hear the young lady's nervous response.

"That's Mrs. Belton, the colonel's wife," said Millicent Lambert.

"Married, eh? A shame. Wonderful golden curls," said Alexander.

"Golden curls?" said Millicent with a giggle. "Oh,

you mean the other one. That's Miss Edgewood. She teaches at the school here in Pixley."

"School?"

"Yes, that short gentleman over there is Mr. Dodwell. He owns the house and lands; Miss Edgewood is his niece. I believe your wards are there, too, my lord."

"My wards? I don't believe I know . . ."

"Abigail and Amanda Heart. They always said you were their guardian, my lord."

"Oh, yes, so I am, and their cousin, too. Why are they not here tonight?"

"They are not yet out. They are only sixteen, you know—just schoolgirls. Hardly appropriate guests for a ball."

"I see," he said, leering down at the pretty girl and causing her to blush. "You, however, are very much out. Correct, Miss Lambert?"

"La, my lord, I have been out this age."

Leaning over her shoulder as he seated her at the table, the earl murmured, "I could tell the minute I laid eyes on you, my dear Miss Lambert."

Grace watched from across the table as Millie went white and then red, her eyes glued to the table. Wicked man! she thought, her gaze riveted on the older man. Why, he was almost old enough to be Millie's father. What was Mrs. Lambert thinking to seat her daughter next to such a man? Even here in Pixley, the reputation of the Earl of Foxworth was legend. The man was a rake, a womanizer. The last thing Millie needed was to be thrown into company with such a man.

Grace blanched when she realized the earl had put his quizzing glass to his eye and was studying her. The man was incorrigible! He had no scruples at all!

He dropped the glass and smiled at her, his dark eyes—so like his brother's—looking into her mind. She lifted her chin and glared at him. He lifted his wine goblet, raising his brows in challenge. Grace put her own glass to her lips and drank deeply, never taking her eyes from his.

The earl returned his glass to the table, his amusement showing in his handsome face. Grace couldn't help but answer that smile in kind, but she became disconcerted when he laced his fingers and peered at her over his knuckles. He was assessing her, that much she could tell, but she didn't want to speculate as to his purpose.

A quick glance down the table, and Grace discovered another pair of eyes studying her, only the reason for this gaze was easy to divine. Adam Havenhurst was furious, his angry glare shifting from her to his brother and back again.

Well, let him fume! She had done nothing wrong! How dare he sit in judgment of her. He should be admonishing his brother—flirting with a girl of Millicent Lambert's tender years.

"Miss Edgewood, isn't it?"

The deep voice, so like the vicar's, intruded into her thoughts, and Grace gasped in surprise.

Mrs. Lambert was looking daggers at her as the earl continued blithely. "I know this is a formal dinner, but this is such a convivial gathering, I'm sure Mrs. Lambert won't mind if we bend the rules and converse with others besides our immediate neighbors." The rake smiled at Millie on his right before reaching across the table, taking Mrs. Lambert's hand, and giving it an intimate squeeze. "They are such charming dinner companions, but I do so enjoy hearty discussions."

"Of course, my lord. What an excellent idea." With this, their charmed hostess threw out all her carefully coordinated place settings, and tapped her crystal wine goblet until she had all eyes on her. Swallowing nervously, she glanced at the instigator, who threw her another charismatic grin, and plunged into speech. "My dear friends, Lord Foxworth has made an excellent proposal, which I heartily endorse. It would be a shame to limit our conversation to the people on our left or right, so we will bend the stodgy rules of polite company and make our conversation general. I do hope you will enjoy your meal," she said, accepting the kiss the earl bestowed on the back of her hand as her due.

The young people were delighted; the older people were distracted, but smiled and tried to make the best of it. Grace was wondering how in the world she could speak to Adam when he was not only across the table, but five people down the row. Not that she really wanted to address any remarks to him until he had apologized, she told herself. Besides, his audacious brother was determined to capture her attention.

Finally, Grace resigned herself to conversation with the earl. His choice of topics surprised her at first, leading her to lower her guard.

"I understand you have my dear wards at your school," he began.

"Your wards? Oh, Abigail and Amanda. Yes, they have been with us for some time. First, they lived at home, but since their mother has gone abroad, they now live at Dodwell Academy."

"How delightful for them," said the rake. "I understand from Miss Lambert that you have a very unusual school." Delivering this statement with an appealing smile for Millie, her mother, and Grace, the earl captivated his audience.

"Yes, I believe it is, but we have the usual courses of study. No young lady should finish school without the rudimentary foundations in mathematics, geography, and language. Not to mention the requisite dancing, music, and art. My uncle is an accomplished artist in his own right and is an excellent dancer. Mrs. Stiles teaches music to the girls."

"And you, Miss Edgewood. What do you teach?"

"I teach the sciences, archery, riding, and swimming."

"Swimming? I am amazed," said the earl. "I would have thought it too cold to swim most of the year."

"Oh, they have a lovely bathhouse," said Millie Lambert. "It is huge, with stone fireplaces that keep it nice and warm."

"That is quite enough, Millicent. Bathhouses, indeed," said her mother. "I hope you will forgive my daughter speaking about such an intimate subject, my lord. She is still young and doesn't realize her conversation is so provocative—entirely unsuitable for polite company."

"Of course," said the earl, leaning toward the mother for an intimate smile. "I applaud your modesty, madam. We will speak no more of it tonight. But, Miss Edgewood, I hope you will allow me to come and see you tomorrow to better discuss what is suitable for my wards."

Inwardly seething, Grace smiled and nodded, saying, "Certainly, my lord. You are welcome at Dodwell Academy at any time. I'm sure your wards will enjoy renewing their acquaintance with you."

Grace turned to Mr. Crane, who was on her left, and forced her way into his conversation with Mrs. Brough. Anything to keep from being dragged back into discussion with the arrogant earl.

How like his younger brother he was!

Dinner was interminable, or so it seemed to Adam, who had been abandoned to his own fate, between Miss Silverton and the clinging Lady Briscoe. Glancing around the table like a trapped animal, his gaze fell again on Grace Edgewood. She was quite engrossed in conversation with that Crane fellow, occasionally including Lord Briscoe, who was already in his cups.

She was a vision in that gown. With her full figure, the fact that her neckline was too high to reveal her ample charms made it all the more enticing. The dark color of the gown was becoming to her complexion, and her hair shone like the gown's golden threads, gleaming in the candlelight. She had pulled her short curls back into a little nest of ringlets at the crown of her head, lending her the profile of a Greek goddess.

Oh, he really had to stop torturing himself in this manner, he thought, tearing his gaze away, only to find Miss Silverton ready to pounce once again.

The ball thrown in honor of his arrival in Pixley was rapidly becoming a nightmare!

Finally, Mrs. Lambert rose and signaled to the other ladies that they would leave the gentlemen to their port. Adam watched their departure with relief. He had had his fill of seeing Miss Edgewood disport herself like a . . .

"You know, brother, if I had known how fascinating the inhabitants of your little parish were, I would have visited long ago."

"You mean the ladies, Alex, and you are making a cake of yourself, flirting with a girl young enough to be your daughter."

"Who? Miss Lambert? I assure you, old boy, she's not the one who has caught my eye. Sometimes I wonder about you, Adam. Has your devotion blinded you? It must have done if you haven't noticed Miss Edgewood's charm and beauty."

"I have noticed," said Adam, grinding his teeth. "But I am not some predatory animal on the prowl."

"So you've noticed her. Very well, then I will back off and give you a chance. Once you muddle it up, I'll step in."

With this, the earl strolled out of the room, heading toward the salon where the ladies were gathered. Adam put down his glass and followed.

"Adam, dear!" called his mother when he entered the

salon. With a grimace, he walked toward her while watching as his older brother was surrounded by several of the older women, including Mrs. Lambert, who dragged Millicent into the ring.

"I don't see how you can bear to live in this primitive place. Why, half the people here tonight are shopkeepers! And the others are mere schoolteachers!"

"Mother, these people are members of my parish. If our hostess considers them suitable for her drawing room, I'm sure you should have nothing to say on the matter."

"Never say you think it proper for Miss Silverton to be here. Why, her grandmother was nothing but a lady's maid."

"And Brummell's grandfather was a valet, Mother, but you were quite willing to meet him in public."

"That's different. He was in the prince's pocket back then. Only see what good came of it," said the dowager, lifting her lorgnette and staring down her nose at the assemblage. Her gaze came to rest on Grace, and she sniffed. "That one, I'm told, prances around in next to nothing, teaching swimming, of all things!"

"Mother, enough of this."

"Surely you don't condone such immoral behavior? You, a vicar!" she said, tossing her turbaned head. "What's more, I heard her tell Lady Briscoe that she is thinking of adding fencing to the curriculum. When I get home tonight, I shall write to your cousin Amelia—you know, her daughters are at that school—and inform her of the scandalous goings-on at Dodwell Academy."

"I wish you would not, Mother. I . . . I will speak to Miss Edgewood. I'm sure she was only teasing about the fencing. I believe she likes to shock people."

"Shock people? What sort of character does that reveal in a young woman? I think you should have nothing to do with her, Adam. You do not want to be accused of condoning such disgraceful behavior."

"Mother, I . . ." Words deserted him, and Adam stalked away, slipping through the open doors to recapture his equanimity. His mother was enough to try the patience of a saint, and as he was nowhere near sainthood, he found her conversation offensive and dangerous. While he might choose to debate with Miss Edgewood the morality of teaching girls to swim and fence, he had no desire to listen to his mother pronouncing judgment.

The musicians, who had been placed in an alcove in the drawing room, began tuning their instruments. Other guests, not invited to dinner, were being announced, and the servants opened the row of doors leading to the terrace to allow the cool air inside. Adam knew he needed to return to the house, but the crisp autumn air was like a tonic, and he lingered on the terrace until he heard the musicians strike up the first tune. Listening to the music, Adam turned and found himself facing Grace Edgewood, her figure highlighted by the soft glow of candlelight shining from the drawing room.

"Good evening, Miss Edgewood," he said, stepping toward her.

"Good evening, Mr. Havenhurst," she replied, smiling at him.

"I was just returning to the house," he said, looking away.

"It is very crowded in there. Mrs. Lambert is having the servants roll up the carpets from the great hall so some people can dance out there, too. It seems everyone wanted to come meet the new vicar," she added, looking up at him, her face only inches from his.

"It's a waltz, I think," he said stupidly, and she nodded. "Would you do me the honor?"

Her smile brightened, and she nodded, taking his hand

and allowing him to twirl her around the terrace. Adam held her quite properly, but still, she was in his arms, and the scent of her perfume—lavender, he guessed—was enough to drive him wild. He breathed deeply, gazing down at her and thinking how very lovely she was.

"Thank you," said Grace.

Startled by her response, Adam realized he had spoken the words out loud. He shook himself mentally; this would never do. He was much too sensible to be uttering such drivel . . . not that she wasn't lovely.

"I have been wanting to apologize again, Miss Edgewood. I don't know what came over me."

She had the audacity to remove her hand from his shoulder and touch his lips, saying, "Please do not, Mr. Havenhurst. Our apologies always seem to end in fresh arguments."

"Very well, then perhaps I should just speak to you about my concerns over what you are teaching your students." He could feel her stiffen in his arms. This was not going to go smoothly, but he could not back down now. "You know, I believe many people think this bathhouse business is completely improper."

"Do they?" she asked sweetly.

Adam nodded, glad that she was taking it so well. Perhaps now she was coming around to his point of view. What a relief, especially since a number of other couples had found their way onto the terrace for the waltz, too.

With a smile, he continued. "Yes, there has been talk, and I must say, I agree. I mean, surely you know that it is improper, perhaps even immoral, for girls to be cavorting about in next to nothing. Why, anyone might see them," he added, warming to his theme.

Adam stumbled as Grace stopped in midstep.

"Please tell me what bothers you, precisely, about my teaching our girls to swim, Mr. Havenhurst," she said, standing as still as a statue.

"Please, Miss Edgewood, everyone is staring." He tried to take her hand again, but she jerked it away, her eyes blazing.

"I insist, sir, that you explain your concern about our bathhouse. You say the girls wear next to nothing. How do you know what they are wearing?"

Her voice grew even louder so that it carried beyond the terrace and into the drawing room. Several couples stopped dancing and stood by the doors, avidly watching and listening as if they were attending a play.

"Miss Edgewood, I just mean that it is unseemly for young ladies to dress . . . or rather, not to dress . . . I mean, there are windows, and . . ." said Adam, wishing he could vanish into a puff of smoke. Whatever was the matter with him? There was no way he was going to win this argument; he was only making a fool of himself.

"True, Mr. Havenhurst, there are windows. I wonder, however, if the matter is not that there are windows, sir," she continued, enunciating each syllable until it sounded like a volley of guns being fired, "but rather, that they are set too high—as you know only too well from your own experience—to allow you to gawk at the girls in their bathing costumes."

The accusation was ludicrous; it required his denial. Instead, his jaw dropped, and words failed him. Adam turned on his heel and stalked away, ignoring the flurry of laughter from the other occupants of the terrace.

It would be all over the village tomorrow, thought Grace, her breasts heaving with indignation while she swayed back and forth, still incapable of movement. Stepping out of the shadows, the amused Earl of Foxworth took her arm to lead her back inside the drawing room.

Bending his head to speak directly into her ear, he whispered, "Bravo, my dear. The man deserved to be put in his place."

Grace looked up at him, her eyes filling with tears at this show of support. It was ever so; when she was angry, tears sprang to her eyes, making people think they had the upper hand. At least this time she had waited until the sanctimonious Mr. Havenhurst was out of sight.

Turning so that his broad shoulders shielded her from the curious gazes of the other guests, the earl took his handkerchief and proceeded to wipe away her tears, his touch light and gentle."There, there, my dear. I assure you, my brother isn't worth it. You should simply ignore him; I always do. And this time, he doesn't know what he's talking about," said the earl.

"Do you really think so, my lord? You don't think my teaching the girls to swim is so outrageous? I mean, if your daughter were to find herself thrown from her horse into a swirling river, you would certainly be thankful if she had learned to swim, wouldn't you?"

"Of course, my dear. Why, I think what you're doing is positively noble. Don't let that priggish brother of mine tell you any differently!" he added, putting a bracing arm around her shoulders as he turned her to face the ball-room. The Earl of Foxworth smiled and nodded at his brother, who was looking daggers at them from across the room.

Six

When the next dance began, it seemed only natural for the Earl of Foxworth to ask Grace to join him. He had remained by her side, speaking of inconsequential things, his company providing just the diversion Grace so sorely needed. Every so often, she would look about her, spy the vicar, and toss her head, her nose firmly in the air. Each time she did this, the earl laughed as if she had uttered some great witticism.

He was without a doubt the most imposing figure in the room. Not even Adam could hold a candle to his brother, with his dark eyes and dark, wavy hair. He was taller than the vicar, too, and Grace found she had to look up at him. He was, she judged, as tall as her brother James. His size made her feel rather petite, and Grace decided she liked the feeling as she met him in the figures of the dance once again.

"Perhaps you will allow me to call on you tomorrow, Miss Edgewood," he said, squeezing her hand.

"I understood you planned to do so, my lord, to see your wards," said Grace, smiling up at him before the steps separated them again.

Moments later, the earl picked up their conversation as if they had never parted. "Ah, yes, so I shall, but I hoped you might be available for a drive. It has been

Take a Trip Back to the Romantic Regent Era of the Early 1800's with

4 FREE
Zebra Regency Romances!

(A $19.96 VALUE!)

4 FREE books are yours!

PLUS YOU'LL SAVE ALMOST $4.00 EVERY MONTH WITH CONVENIENT HOME DELIVERY!

We'd Like to Invite You to Subscribe to Zebra's Regency Romance Book Club and Give You a Gift of 4 Free Books as Your Introduction! *(Worth $19.96!)*

If you're a Regency lover, imagine the joy of getting **4 FREE Zebra Regency Romances** and then the chance to have these lovely stories delivered to your home each month at the lowest price available! Well, that's our offer to you and here's how you benefit by becoming a Regency Romance subscriber:

- 4 FREE Introductory Regency Romances are delivered to your doorstep (you only pay for shipping and handling)

- 4 BRAND NEW Regencies are then delivered each month (usually before they're available in bookstores)

- Subscribers save almost $4.00 every month

- You also receive a **FREE** monthly newsletter, which features author profiles, discounts, subscriber benefits, book previews and more

- No risks or obligations...in other words, you can cancel whenever you wish with no questions asked

Join the thousands of readers who enjoy the savings and convenience offered to Regency Romance subscribers. After your initial introductory shipment, you receive 4 brand-new Zebra Regency Romances each month to examine for 10 days. Then, if you decide to keep the books, you'll pay the preferred subscriber's price, plus shipping and handling.

It's a no-lose proposition, so return the FREE BOOK CERTIFICATE today!

Say Yes to 4 Free Books!
Complete and return the order card to receive this $19.96 value, ABSOLUTELY FREE!

If the certificate is missing below, write to:
Regency Romance Book Club
P.O. Box 5214, Clifton, New Jersey 07015-5214
or call TOLL-FREE 1-800-770-1963
Visit our website at www.kensingtonbooks.com.

FREE BOOK CERTIFICATE

YES! Please rush me 4 Zebra Regency Romances (I only pay for shipping and handling). I understand that each month thereafter I will be able to preview 4 brand-new Regency Romances FREE for 10 days. Then, if I should decide to keep them, I will pay the money-saving preferred subscriber's price for all 4...that's a savings of 20% off the publisher's price. I may return any shipment within 10 days and owe nothing, and I may cancel this subscription at any time. My 4 FREE books will be mine to keep in any case.

Name _____

Address _____ Apt. _____

City _____ State _____ Zip _____

Telephone ( ) _____

Signature _____
(If under 18, parent or guardian must sign.)

RN072A

Terms and prices subject to change. Orders subject to acceptance by Regency Romance Book Club.
Offer valid in U.S. only.

Treat yourself to 4 FREE Regency Romances!

A
$19.96
VALUE...
FREE!

No
obligation
to buy
anything,
ever!

PLACE
STAMP
HERE

ll...l..lll....llll..l.l.l.l..l..l..l.l.l..lll..lll...l

REGENCY ROMANCE BOOK CLUB
Zebra Home Subscription Service, Inc.
P.O. Box 5214
Clifton NJ 07015-5214

years since I have visited Pixley, and I thought you might show me around."

"I would be delighted, but you will have to wait until late in the afternoon, my lord. I do have my classes to teach."

The music ended, and he bowed to her, taking her hand to help her rise from her curtsy. For a moment, she thought he meant to kiss her hand, but he released it with a lingering sigh.

"Shall we say five o'clock?"

"That would be wonderful," said Grace, turning to find Mr. Crane waiting to claim her hand for the next set.

The evening became a blur of partners. Everyone wanted to know precisely what she and the new vicar had quarreled about. Each gentleman tried to glean the facts without asking directly, and by the time the evening was coming to a close, the story was stretched to the breaking point.

Alarmed, Margaret Stiles pulled Grace to one side to demand the truth.

"Margaret, I am sick to death of being interrogated about it. Mr. Havenhurst does not approve of my teaching the girls to swim. I told him I didn't care, and that was the end of it," said Grace, gritting her teeth in annoyance.

"Well, everyone is saying that you accused Mr. Havenhurst of trying to molest the girls while they were swimming," whispered her friend.

"Nonsense, it was no such thing. You know how strongly I feel about the girls being physically fit, besides the benefit of knowing how to swim," said Grace, turning away and finding herself face-to-face with a very inebriated Lord Briscoe waiting for the next dance, a waltz.

"All I can say is, you give 'im a muffler, Miss Edgewood," said the viscount, swaying as he took her into his arms. "Or if you want me to tell him for you, just say the word."

"Tell who, my lord? And what am I to tell him? I'm afraid I don't understand," she said, looking down at the short man who was staring directly at her bosom. He dragged his eyes upward and grinned, winking at her. Grace looked away, her face turning beet red when she encountered Adam Havenhurst watching this byplay, his dark eyes soft with sympathy. She wanted very much to run away and hide.

"Adam, that's who. My old friend," said the viscount. "He always was one to go sticking his oar in where it wasn't needed. I heard what he said to you out there on the terrace, an' then I heard what you said to the earl, an' I agree. You just go ahead and teach my little, uh . . . my . . ."

"Ellen?" she supplied.

"Yes, that's it! Teach my little Ellen to swim. I don't want her drowning in a river."

With this, he started to cry—loud, wet sobs, and his weight shifted so that she was practically dragging him around the room. Grace could feel all eyes on them, and she tried her best to guide him off the dance floor. Suddenly he stumbled, and his face rammed into her chest, knocking the breath out of her. Her desperation turned to relief when she saw Adam start toward her. He would save her. Then he stopped, and Grace frowned.

"Allow me, Miss Edgewood." The Earl of Foxworth grabbed the viscount under the arms and lifted him off her.

Devil take the man, thought Grace.

"A bit too much to drink," announced the earl, diffusing the situation with a ready laugh. He practically carried the viscount out of the drawing room and into the hall.

Grace hesitated, glancing at Adam, who was looking decidedly stormy. No doubt he thought she deserved the viscount's show of bad manners, she thought dismally.

Lifting her chin defiantly, Grace followed the earl, calling loudly for the viscount's hat.

In the hall, Lord Briscoe's ever-suffering wife was thanking the earl profusely while he handed her husband over to a footman.

"Please forgive my husband, Miss Edgewood," she begged.

"Certainly, my lady. Do you need help getting him home?" asked Grace.

"No, no, the coachman will see to him. He promised me tonight . . . but there you have it. It is not that he drinks so very much, you know," she said, her eyes pleading for their understanding. "It is just that it takes so little to put him in this state."

"He'll be fine in the morning, and I'm sure no one will even remember it," said the earl.

"Thank you again," said Lady Briscoe, allowing the earl to help her into the carriage. "Please give my excuses to Mrs. Lambert," she said to Grace.

"Certainly. Good night."

They waited a moment while the carriage disappeared into the darkness.

"Well, you've had quite an adventure tonight, Miss Edgewood. Tell me, is Pixley always so lively?"

Grace giggled and shook her head. "No, my lord. I can honestly say that until you and your brother arrived—and your charming mother, too—Pixley was quite dull."

He offered his arm to lead her back inside. "If you think my brother and I have stirred things up, just wait until my mother gets started."

When they entered the drawing room, all eyes turned to watch. Adam, dancing with Mrs. Brough, missed his step and trod heavily on the dressmaker's satin slipper, causing her to let out a shriek.

"My brother was never known for his dancing expertise," said the earl with a deep chuckle.

Grace, who had not taken her eyes from the vicar, said wistfully, "I thought him quite graceful."

"Foxworth, you must speak to your brother," said the countess, ignoring Grace's presence completely as she tugged on her older son's sleeve.

"I often speak to Adam, Mother."

"There is no need for your flippancy, Alexander. You know what I mean. Look at him, dancing with that woman," said the countess, who would have been a handsome woman were it not for the ever-present curled lip and sneer that marred her features.

"I'm sure there is nothing wrong with Mrs. Brough," said Grace, frowning in confusion. "She is Mrs. Lambert's sister, you know."

"She is a mere shopkeeper, a seamstress."

"Mother, you are being insulting."

"I am speaking the truth, and you know it. She is welcome to sew a shirt for him—though I venture to say it would be the most unsightly of garments—but she is not the type of woman with whom Adam should be associating."

With this, the countess marched away, bearing down on their hostess as the music came to a close.

"You see what I mean," said the earl.

"Never mean to say she will tell Mrs. Lambert what she told us," exclaimed Grace.

"Oh, not in precisely those terms, but unless Mrs. Lambert is thick-headed, she will get the gist of it. I am sorry, Miss Edgewood, but I believe it is time to take my family and go home for the evening. It has been a pleasure, and I look forward to our drive tomorrow afternoon. Good night," he said, bowing over her hand.

"Good night, my lord," said Grace, watching as the

earl signaled to his brother. Together, they bore down on their mother and said their farewells to their hostess.

It was the signal for the gathering to break up. The young people were still enjoying themselves, but the older revelers, who had attended just because the new vicar and the Earl of Foxworth were attending, began their exodus as well.

"I suppose we should go." Mrs. Stiles sighed, appearing at Grace's side.

"I think it would be for the best. We have school tomorrow," said Grace.

"True. If we had thought aright, we would have canceled classes for tomorrow as well as today."

Grace laughed and moved away to round up Pamela, Diana, and Olivia. Stepping onto the terrace, she encountered the vicar instead. She thought he had already left. Before she could take flight, he put a gentle hand on her arm.

"Miss Edgewood, I could not leave without straightening out this misunderstanding."

"I don't believe there is a misunderstanding, Mr. Havenhurst," she said wearily. "You seem to think I am Beelzebub himself; I choose to think I am merely preparing my students for any eventuality."

"But as your vicar, I am responsible for your mortal soul. Please, Miss Edgewood, may I call on you tomorrow afternoon?"

"Perhaps on Saturday, Mr. Havenhurst. I am engaged to drive out with your brother tomorrow afternoon. If you will excuse me?" she asked, looking down at her arm, where his hand still rested, burning a hole through the thin fabric.

"Certainly" he replied, his nostrils flaring slightly. "Good evening."

* * *

"You've hardly said a word all the way home, Adam, and you still haven't answered my question," said his mother, her voice an irritating whine in the dim light of the carriage.

"No, Mother, I am not coming back to Foxworth Manor with you. I live at the vicarage, and we have been through all that. I do wish you would quit trying to change my mind."

"You can't blame her, Adam. The vicarage is ghastly. I can't imagine anyone, especially my brother, who is accustomed to the finest things in life, choosing to remain there a minute longer than is absolutely necessary," said the earl, stretching his legs and expelling a bored groan.

"Don't you start, Alex. You've only been here two days, and I've had just about enough of you already."

"My, my, what has you up in the boughs?"

"Never mind," snapped Adam, throwing open the carriage door as they pulled up outside the vicarage. "Good night."

"Good night, my dear. Sleep well. Do you have enough blankets?" asked his mother.

Adam signaled the coachman to depart, not bothering to reply. With a weary tread, he entered the little vicarage, glad he had chosen it, despite its limited size. At least it was his.

The hour was late, but nothing compared to the evenings he had spent in London, gadding about from one entertainment to another. That was before he had taken holy orders, becoming a curate at a small church in the City. There, his duties had precluded joining the whirl of social activities to which his birthright and wealth entitled him. At times, working with the poor had been thankless and backbreaking, but he had felt needed for the first time in his life—not the kind of needed his mother wanted him to feel. Her need to smother him had been one of the reasons he had left home in the first place. Tending to the sick and destitute in a hovel in the center of London was one place he could be sure his mother would not venture.

Adam strolled through the tiny house and out the back door to check on Caesar. The horse raised his head and whickered to acknowledge his presence.

"Sleep well, old man," he said, closing the stable door again.

He climbed the stairs to his own bed and undressed, throwing himself onto the counterpane, shirtless, wearing only his unmentionables.

The harvest moon shone through the windows, making it seem like daylight. He wondered idly if Miss Edgewood was looking out her window at that very moment. The smile this image evoked faded away; she was going driving with his brother.

His brother—the rake.

If she were not so angry with him, he would warn her, caution her, but that was what had gotten him into trouble with the headstrong Miss Edgewood in the first place.

No, he would stay out of it—even if to do so was pure torture.

Grace found sleep impossible. Every time she cleared her mind of the uncomfortable memories of Adam's hurtful words or the embarrassment of the viscount's head colliding with her chest, she would recall how very handsome the vicar looked in his black evening clothes. There had been no mended cravat tonight; his dress had been impeccable. And each time he had glanced her way at dinner, his dark brown eyes had burned their way into her soul. His anger had been palpable, and she had persuaded herself that he was jealous over her flirtation with his brother. She should have known better. More than likely, he was worrying that she might corrupt his brother, the worst rake in all of England.

Grace turned over, pulling the counterpane up to her chin with uncommon energy. This vicar was becoming a thorn in her side—robbing her of sleep and tarnishing her reputation with his accusations of impropriety. What was worse, her stomach filled with butterflies at the very thought of those dark, smoldering eyes. No man had ever made her feel so . . . She struggled for the word. Confused did not encompass enough of what she felt when she thought of Adam Havenhurst.

Sitting, Grace drew her knees up, hugging them as she frowned into the darkness.

"Flustered," she whispered. "Flustered and restless and . . . lovesick."

Grace's quiet gasp was followed by a thoughtful smile. Everything was suddenly crystal clear, and a great peace coming over her at the acknowledgment. In the little time since his arrival, Adam Havenhurst had touched her heart in a way no other man had ever done—or was like to do, she admitted with wonder.

The frown reappeared.

Grace Edgewood was a woman of great determination. When she truly wanted something to happen, she moved heaven and earth to see that it did. But her experience with men was very limited. She didn't count her brothers. That was different.

She knew Adam was attracted to her; she had guessed as much. But how did one progress from attraction to love and all the wonderful expectations it entailed?

Just then, there was a knock on her door, followed by Margaret Stiles's head appearing in the opening.

"Are you asleep, my dear?"

"No, I'm afraid not. I shall be quite exhausted tomorrow, or should I say today? We really should have canceled lessons for the day."

"I quite agree," said Margaret, padding silently into the room and drawing a chair up to the bedside, evidently settling in for a cozy chat.

"Did you enjoy yourself tonight, Margaret?"

"I truly did, though my evening was not as exciting as yours," said the older woman coyly. At five-and-forty, Margaret Stiles was ever an incurable romantic, and though her own quest remained unfulfilled, she still cherished hope within her breast.

"Exciting is hardly the word for my evening," said Grace, "but yours, Margaret. Why, I saw you dancing twice with Uncle Rhodes—the waltz, no less. However did you manage to wrest him away from Mrs. Lambert and Mrs. Brough?"

Her friend chortled happily and said, "I don't mind admitting to you, dear; I was quite shameless. I kept Mrs. Lambert busy, dropping hints that the earl was perhaps keeping too close a watch on her daughter. She didn't dare let the girl out of her sight."

Grace laughed, too, and asked, "And what of Mrs. Brough? You know, I've often suspected she entertains ideas about Uncle."

"Oh, it's as plain as the nose on your face, but she's none too sure about him. Besides, with Mr. Crane living in the village, he is a much likelier candidate. She has competition there, of course, in Miss Silverton, as I was only too willing to point out at every opportunity tonight."

"You are quite, quite wicked, Margaret," said Grace.

"A lady must look to herself, and I'm growing weary of waiting."

Grace could see that her friend's brave front was slipping, and she patted her hand sympathetically, and said, "I have never understood why a lady must wait for the man to drop the handkerchief, so to speak. I mean, what

would be so wrong about a lady simply telling a man
how she felt about him?"

"There's nothing wrong with your idea, my dear, but
it would be fatal to do so. Nothing would guarantee failure more quickly."

"That makes no sense," said Grace, frowning fiercely.
"I mean, if I knew I were in love with a man, why
couldn't I just tell him?"

"You could, but he would probably turn tail and run.
In my experience, which I freely admit is very limited,
men do not like being pursued."

"Well, I think it is nonsense, all nonsense," said Grace,
dangerously close to tears.

Now it was Margaret's turn to console her young
friend. They knew each other too well, and Grace had
no need to confess her feelings for Adam. Margaret rose,
giving Grace a fierce hug. Releasing her, Margaret appeared thoughtful, worrying her lower lip until a smile
began to light her face.

"What is it?"

"You know, Grace, one way to pique a man's interest
is to awaken a sense of jealousy in him. My sister did
just that before she married her husband. It turned the
trick for her."

"But, Margaret, that's so . . . dishonest."

"Oh, not really. I mean, it's up to him to decide if you
are worth being jealous over."

"But who could I find . . ." Grace's eyes grew wide
at her friend's smiling nod. "Oh, Margaret, I couldn't!
Why, his reputation alone would be enough to ruin
mine."

"Nonsense! Everyone saw how taken he was with you
tonight. Everyone will assume the famous London rake
has met his match."

"But he is Adam's brother," whispered Grace with a
grimace.

"Precisely," replied Margaret, nodding her head and smiling knowingly.

Grace shook her head vehemently, saying, "I couldn't, Margaret. Truly I could not."

"Mother insisted that I come over and fetch you for nuncheon," said the Earl of Foxworth, spearing another slice of ham and a boiled potato. "Of course, I had no idea your Mrs. Odstock was such an excellent cook. Perhaps I shall steal her away from you."

The old crone beamed at the compliment and actually laughed, though the sound was rusty, like a metal latch in need of oil.

"I couldn't leave the vicar, my lord. But you're welcome anytime in my kitchen," she said, bobbing a quick curtsy.

"And a loyal heart, too. I ask you, brother, what more could you want?"

"A bit of peace and quiet," muttered Adam, pushing away from the table. "I need to go over to the church. Mrs. Lambert was bringing in some girls to clean and polish. I should go over and thank them."

"Wait a minute. I'll walk with you," said the earl, winking broadly at the housekeeper as he picked up a slice of bread, making a quick sandwich with his ham. "I wanted to talk to you anyway."

"Suit yourself," grumbled Adam.

They walked along in silence until they had shut the front gate. Then Alex demanded, "What the deuce has you in such a foul mood today? At least I didn't bring our dear mother with me."

"I know, I know, and I'm thankful for that, but . . . it's something other."

"Come now, little brother, you can tell me. I'm the one who used to sort out all your troubles."

Adam stopped in the middle of the road, shaking his head in disbelief. "You really think that, don't you, Alex? Has it ever occurred to you that most of the tight spots I have been in are due to your influence? Devil take you, man, you were the worst example a young man, green and untried, could have. No matter what I did, I couldn't live up to your legend."

Quite pleased, Alex said, "Legend? I like that. I have never thought of myself as a legend."

"Well, you needn't feel flattered. I didn't mean it as a compliment," grumbled Adam. "Trying to live up to your reputation kept me in constant danger of getting shot by some jealous husband, or killed in a duel, or having some woman run over me with her horse."

"Devil a bit! I refuse to take the blame for that one, Adam. If you hadn't been so ham-fisted as to pursue your own mistress's sister . . . You certainly didn't learn that from me!"

At this, Adam began to laugh, and Alex joined in. They had to move to the side of the road quickly as the Lambert boy sped by on his high-perch phaeton. He threw them a puzzled frown, and Alex groaned. It would be another tale to tell, how the vicar and his lordly brother were standing in the middle of the road, laughing like want-witted jinglebrains.

"Back then, you had about as much sense as that young coxcomb," said Alex, nodding after the speeding vehicle. "I tried and tried, but you never were a dab hand with the ladies."

"I almost got away with it," said Adam, chuckling. "But they looked so demmed much alike in the fog that day, I wasn't sure which one I had hold of. If only I hadn't called her sister's name . . ."

"That's what endearments are for, you cawker! Keeps a fellow from using the wrong name if you call every one of them angel or darling," said the earl, clapping his brother on the back and continuing toward the church. He paused, looking back at his younger brother, who was staring at the ground.

"Is that what you call Miss Edgewood?" asked Adam.

The earl frowned and shook his head. "I call her Miss Edgewood, Adam. I haven't yet decided about her."

"What do you mean by that?" demanded Adam, his hands doubled into fists.

"Just what I said. I haven't decided about Miss Edgewood, but don't worry. I should have a better idea after our drive this afternoon."

"She's a lady, Alex, an unmarried lady," Adam added, his voice soft and stern.

"Is she? I thought she was a schoolmistress." Alexander Havenhurst shrugged his broad shoulders and took a bite out of the sandwich he held. Turning, he strode toward the small church, entering through the front doors.

Adam hurried after him, his fists still doubled.

"Good morning, Vicar!" called Mrs. Lambert, looking up from the altar, where she was arranging a crisp white cloth.

"Good morning, ladies," he said, noting that his profligate brother was already in conversation with the prettiest maid, leaning against a pew while she dusted the dark wood, her telltale blush visible even in the dimly lit church.

It would do no good to remonstrate with Alex, he knew. His only hope would be to warn Miss Edgewood about Alex's rakish reputation. Judging from the way she listened, his warning could prove downright dangerous!

"Good afternoon, my lord," said Abigail and Amanda Heart in unison as they curtsied to their guardian that afternoon.

"Good morning, ladies. I trust you are well," he said formally, indicating that they should sit down on the sofa opposite his chair.

"Very well, my lord," said Abigail.

"Good, I am glad to hear it. I spoke to your mother last month before she went to France. She was glad to know that my brother would be here to help keep an eye on you."

"The vicar is a very kind man," said Abigail, her voice worshipful, a fact that was not lost on the earl.

He raised his brow in query to Grace, who sat in another chair. She grinned at him, but did not explain.

Instead, Grace rose, causing him to stand also. "I will leave you alone with your cousins. You may have private matters to discuss."

"Please do stay, Miss Edgewood. You may be able to add something to my inquiries."

"I believe the girls would speak more freely if I am out of the room, my lord. I will return in twenty minutes. I'll have our housekeeper make up a tea tray. Amanda, you may pour out for your cousin."

"Yes, miss."

"Twenty minutes," he said, giving her an admiring glance as she passed in front of him and made her way to the drawing room door.

"Miss Edgewood is very pretty," said Abigail, whose experience on the cliff had only temporarily subdued her.

"Yes, she is," said the earl, smiling at both girls. They were female, after all—nothing he couldn't handle. "And so are the two of you. I can tell already that you will turn many heads when you go to London for your first Season. Let's see, how old are the two of you now? Sixteen, isn't it?" he added, remembering Millicent Lambert's condescending mention of his wards as being mere children of sixteen.

"Yes," said Abigail, "but I'm surprised you remember."

"Well, we are more than guardian and wards, are we not? You are my cousins, too, and when the time is right, I hope you and your mother will come to stay with me in London. We'll have a grand ball in honor of your come-out."

Amanda, the quiet twin, clapped her hands, but her sister cocked her head to one side and asked, "Miss Edgewood said you were coming today to ask us about our studies, my lord, but you haven't even mentioned them."

"Miss Edgewood has told me all about the subjects you study here, Abigail. I have no desire to make you recite your Latin declensions."

Amanda let out a sigh of relief, and Abigail brightened, too. The housekeeper entered with a tea tray, and the rest of their visit was passed pleasantly, with the earl relating old gossip, of a rather tame variety, about the fashionables of London.

When Grace returned, they were laughing like old friends. Even Amanda, who was usually so shy with strangers, was giggling and conversing easily. Grace met the earl's bland gaze with a smile. He certainly lived up to his reputation; he had to be one of the most engaging men she had ever encountered.

And here she was, intending to use him to make his own brother jealous. The idea was ludicrous. It was the stuff of the stage, and she was certainly not heroine material. Why, except for her brothers, she had spent very little time in the company of gentlemen. She knew next to nothing about flirtation.

Just then, the earl laughed out loud at something his young cousin said. The sound was like the Sirens in mythology; it drew one in, made a person want to be within the circle of his conversation. Grace shook herself. What nonsense was poisoning her brain? When all was said and done, the Earl of Foxworth was only a man.

"Come in, Miss Edgewood, and join us," he said, rising and holding out his hand in invitation.

Grace ignored the shiver of excitement this gesture triggered and moved toward the handsome rake.

No, she thought, she was not a gullible schoolgirl, but she would have to be on her toes to resist the attractive earl. Adam's charm, when he was not being quite impossibly exasperating, was honest and true. The earl's charm was practiced and perfectly suited to a London drawing room, but she was certain it would prove tiresome, living with it every day.

"My dear Miss Edgewood, you have done a marvelous job with my cousins. I find them utterly delightful," said the earl, his comments bringing smiles to the faces of all three of his listeners.

Yes, if her plan was to meet with success, thought Grace, she would need to remind herself often that it was not the earl's heart, but the heart of the vicar she wanted to win.

Was it not?

Seven

Sunset surprised Grace by arriving much earlier that evening—or so it seemed. When in the company of a charming man who was bent on entertaining her, time was soon forgotten, and the sun slipped beyond the horizon before she knew it. Certainly, Grace hadn't planned to miss dinner at the school, but she could not fault herself too much. The Earl of Foxworth was a man of great depth, a fact that surprised and worried her. She had not expected to enjoy their drive so very much. His tales about London intrigued her, too, yet she had always scoffed at the girls who spoke of nothing but balls and routs.

Still, though she found herself drawn to the earl, she was not so taken with him that she forgot her purpose for driving out with him. She kept up her end of the conversation by pointing out every house and every pasture, enumerating the wonders of the village and its environs. He listened attentively, watching her in the most disconcerting manner, his eyes traveling from her eyes to her hair and then her lips. Each time, just as his scrutiny began to make her feel uncomfortable, he would return his attention to the horses.

When they arrived back at the school, they drove past the stone bathhouse, which was awash with light. The older girls had leave to use the pool on Friday night, and their exuberant squeals and splashing made the earl halt his team.

"What a delightful sound," he said, smiling down at Grace. "Young people enjoying themselves. I have two sons, you know. Their laughter is the great joy in my life. Hearing your girls makes me realize how very empty my home is with them away at school.

"I didn't know you had children, my lord."

"Yes, two boys. My wife died in childbirth when Phillip was born."

"I am sorry," said Grace, laying a hand on his sleeve.

He put his hand over hers, giving it a squeeze. Another squeal broke the stillness and the spell. Grace withdrew her hand.

"One can't help but smile," he said with a smile.

"I quite agree," replied Grace, completely in charity with her companion. "I'm glad Mrs. Stiles let the girls have their time tonight. Normally, I am the one who accompanies them to the bathhouse."

"Another thing I must apologize for, I fear, Miss Edgewood," he said, taking her hand and lifting it to his lips while gazing into her eyes. She blushed a fiery red but did not snatch her hand away.

He released her and said in quite normal tones, "I have been thinking of adding a bathhouse to my estate. I would love to see yours one day, if there is a time when the girls are not using it."

"Certainly, my lord. Sunday afternoon, perhaps?"

"Splendid. I look forward to it. Now, I have kept you from your dinner long enough, my dear Miss Edgewood." He picked up the reins and drove to the front door of the house. Their one groom, Patrick, had been waiting, and he held the team while the earl helped Grace down. With only a slight bow over her hand, the earl smiled and was gone, leaving Grace to wander into the house alone.

Solitude was not to be her lot, however, as Margaret Stiles accosted her, dragging her into her uncle's study.

"Really, Margaret, I am too tired, and there is nothing to tell. I went for a drive with the earl . . ."

"A very long drive," said her friend, taking the seat beside Grace on the sofa.

"Yes, a very long drive. I'm afraid the time quite ran away with us. I hope you were not worried, Uncle," said Grace, reaching out and patting his hand.

Dragging his attention away from the book in his lap, he smiled up at her and shook his head. "Certainly not, my dear. I know that you can take care of yourself."

"Thank you. Now, Margaret, I really would like to get something to eat."

Margaret Stiles jumped up and hurried to the bell rope, saying, "I told Mrs. Green to make up a plate for you. I knew you would be hungry. She will bring it in with our tea, my dear."

Uncle Rhodes winked at his niece, and Grace settled back against the cushions, a rueful smile on her face.

"Until you tell her every minute detail, you will be held captive in this room, my dear. You had best get it over with."

Grace whispered loudly, "Do you think she will be satisfied with the truth, or shall I make up something outrageous?"

"I heard that," said Margaret Stiles, returning to the sofa and taking her seat beside Grace. "And of course I want the truth. But tell me, are none of the stories we have heard about the Earl of Foxworth true? I mean, was he a perfect gentleman?"

Margaret could not keep the disappointment out of her voice, and Grace laughed.

"Margaret, surely you didn't want our Grace to have to fight the rogue off of her!" said Rhodes Dodwell, rather shocked at their sweet-tempered friend.

"No, no, of course I did not, but I thought there might have been something in his manner that showed he had actually earned his reputation."

"Well, if being a polite and informative conversationalist is the criteria for being called a rake, then the Earl of Foxworth has indeed earned that title. I assure you, Margaret, he was the perfect gentleman. His manners were just as they ought to be."

"Oh, how nice," said the older woman with a sigh.

"There was one thing . . ."

"Do tell!" exclaimed Margaret, practically bouncing up and down.

Just then the housekeeper entered with the tea tray. Mrs. Stiles shooed her away quickly, but their interesting conversation was postponed until they had all been served.

Grace was allowed to take three bites before Margaret asked with studied casualness, "What was that one thing, my dear?"

"It was probably nothing, but he does have a way of studying a person that is almost . . . disconcerting. But just when I would begin to wonder what he was thinking, staring at me so, he would turn his attention to his horses or the road. Or he would introduce a new topic of conversation. Really, Uncle, you should speak to him about India. Did you know that he lived there for a year?"

"No, I didn't. Well, we must invite his lordship to dinner . . . and his family, too, of course."

Margaret Stiles clapped her hands and began wringing them in anticipation. "When? We shouldn't wait too long. We have no idea how long the earl and his mother plan to stay."

"As to his mother, she plans to stay indefinitely. At least as long as Adam is vicar here."

"Adam?" said Rhodes Dodwell, his attention caught by this one word.

Grace felt a blush steal across her cheeks, but she jutted out her chin and said defiantly, "I am only repeating what his brother said to me. I believe I know better than to address a stranger by his given name."

"Just so," murmured her uncle, but he was not deceived.

Grace could tell by the way he studied her that he didn't believe for a moment that Adam's name had passed her lips for the first time. Well, let him speculate, she thought, feigning a great interest in the apple she was peeling for her dessert. She was past the age of answering to a guardian.

"We will set the dinner party for a week from Saturday. Does that sound about right?"

"Very well, but let us keep it simple," said Rhodes. "Let's not invite half the parish. Let's just keep it to us and them."

"An excellent notion," said Margaret. "It should give the dowager countess less to complain about. She was quite incensed at being forced into the society of shopkeepers."

Grace felt certain the viperish woman would be just as displeased to be sitting down to a small dinner, practically *en famille,* with schoolteachers, but she wisely held her tongue. They were from good families; her eldest brother now held her late father's title of Baron Edgewood, and Margaret's grandfather had been a viscount. And her uncle, her mother's brother, though he held no title, his family could trace its roots back to the days of the Conqueror.

They couldn't help it if they chose to lead productive lives, unlike other members of the *ton* who spent their days in idle splendor. Still, if one cared about such matters, and the countess obviously did, she couldn't object to their bloodlines, as they were certainly a step above tradespeople.

The niggling doubt gnawed at Grace that she would never be acceptable as a daughter-in-law to one such as the Countess of Foxworth, but she refused to allow the thought to cast her down. Why should she? When—and if—she won Adam's heart, then she would worry about the countess.

On this rather somber note, she declared herself exhausted, kissed her uncle's cheek, and said good night, leaving Margaret to stew in her own speculations.

"Here now, Vicar, you're turned out very smart today," said Mrs. Odstock when Adam entered the kitchen the next morning, heading for the stables.

He couldn't help but be pleased by her compliment; it was such a rarity to hear praise of any sort from the sour housekeeper. He had spent all of fifteen minutes tying his cravat, and he wore one of the coats from the trunks his mother had brought. He was hardly a dandy, but he wanted to look his best when he called on Miss Edgewood. Adam hadn't questioned his motives; he had merely acted accordingly.

"Thank you, Mrs. Odstock. I have a few calls to make this morning."

"Ay, I've heard all about it. Calling on Miss Edgewood, according to the smithy Mr. Gray."

Adam was beginning to realize his every activity would be scrutinized so he made no comment as to the accuracy of her observation.

Instead, he said firmly, "As I said, Mrs. Odstock, I have several calls to make."

"Ay, but you might as well forget about calling on Miss Edgewood, if you're hopin' to win her favors. From what young Mr. Lambert told Mr. Crane, Miss Edgewood is anglin' for bigger fish now. I mean, why settle for a vicar when you can have an earl?"

"Good morning to you, Mrs. Odstock," said Adam, carefully closing the door behind him. It would not be seemly for a vicar to slam out of the house, though he found himself overwhelmed with the desire to smash something.

Instead, he clawed at his cravat, which suddenly threatened to strangle him. What did it matter if he was fashionably turned out? His brother and Miss Edgewood—pairing them in his mind was enough to make him grind his teeth—they would make an admirable couple. After all, his brother had no need of a bride with a dowry, and Miss Edgewood would surely enjoy living in the lap of luxury. Who would not? he thought, exacting perfect logic of himself even as his heart twisted in pain.

"Good morning, Vicar," called Miss Silverton.

He raised his whip in salute, causing the usually calm Caesar to pick up his pace as they passed through the village. Old Mr. Thurgood, out for a stroll with his little granddaughter, hobbled quickly to the side of the road as the curricle sped past. There, thought Adam bitterly, another thing for the villagers to talk about, how the new vicar drives like a maniac through the town, running down old men and young children.

The beauty of the day and the cool breeze steadied his outlook as he continued down the country lane. Adam shook his head at his own idiocy. Miss Edgewood and his brother had absolutely nothing in common. Why, Alex had probably been bored beyond belief, spending an afternoon driving with the pretty schoolmistress. And he certainly was not in the market for a wife. On this comforting thought, Adam began to relax.

He found a new appreciation in the crisp autumn air as he tooled his curricle along the empty road, and he decided it would be best to take Miss Edgewood out for a drive. That way, they could be private without risking scandal.

He drove around to the stable yard to leave his carriage with the groom.

"Good morning, Vicar," said Patrick, taking Caesar's head.

"Good morning, Patrick. It's very quiet this morning. I would have thought the girls might be riding."

"Oh, not today. They're all inside listening to each other performing their music. Listen, you can hear them from here." The groom lowered his voice and continued confidentially. "Mind, I think it's very brave of you to come today. Some of the girls are not what I would call blessed with talent in the musical department, if you catch my meaning."

Adam chuckled, but he continued on toward the house. He wished Grace had warned him about this. He would have postponed his visit. As he neared the house, the harpist finished her piece, and he could hear a sweet, childish voice lifted in song. The pianoforte accompanying her occasionally hit a false note, but the singer plowed on with perfect pitch.

Adam shook his head as the pianoforte's notes ended in a resounding, if somewhat flat, crescendo. With a deep breath, he prepared himself to do his duty. Pasting a pleasant smile on his face, he knocked on the door.

"Mr. Havenhurst, what a pleasure this is," said Mrs. Stiles who was lingering in the hall, her head pounding from the strain of the morning.

"Thank you, Mrs. Stiles. I was calling on Miss Edgewood, but Patrick warned . . . that is, he told me there is a recital of sorts going on. I hope the girls won't mind my attending."

"They will be delighted, I'm sure. Won't you step this way?" The older woman cringed as she opened the door to the drawing room; once again, the harp was being tortured instead of the pianoforte, and there was no sweet voice to drown out the sound.

Adam couldn't help wishing he were anywhere else, and then he saw Grace coming toward him, a smile on her face and her hands extended in sincere welcome. She wore a deep purple morning gown that set off her complexion and golden curls to perfection. Her beauty and grace took his breath away, and he wished he hadn't made a mess of his carefully tied cravat.

"You came, Mr. Havenhurst. I am so glad," she said, smiling up at him, her green eyes alight with pleasure. "I do apologize for dragging you into our little musicale," she added in a whisper. "I truly forgot all about it."

"I don't mind at all, Miss Edgewood, if you don't mind my staying and listening."

"Not at all. Please do come in. Let me get you a chair," she said, picking up a dainty chair which he took from her unresisting hands.

Following Grace back to her chair, Adam placed his by her side, all the while smiling like a ninny at the sea of girlish faces watching him instead of the performer.

The next hour was spent listening to one performer after another, some good and some very bad. Through it all, Adam smiled and applauded, offering encouragement and compliments to each girl. His ears might be wounded, but his pleasure knew no bounds with Miss Edgewood by his side, smiling on him in reward for his kindness to her students.

Finally it was over. It was almost time for nuncheon, and though he was a vicar and needed to exercise patience, Adam was certain he would lose his mind if he was forced to listen to one more girlish giggle.

"I was wondering, Miss Edgewood, if we might go for a drive."

"Well, I really should . . ."

"Now, now, Grace, my girl, you run along. Mrs. Stiles and I can certainly handle the girls. It will do you good. And why don't you ask Cook to pack a little picnic for the two of you. It would be a shame to waste this fine weather," said her uncle, giving her a quick buss on the cheek.

"What a splendid idea," said Adam, his fingers crossed behind his back.

"Oh, why not? If you'll wait a few minutes, Mr. Havenhurst?"

"Impatiently," he said with a debonair smile. "But I promise you I shall wait."

With a quick grin that touched him like a kiss, Grace hurried out of the room and up the stairs to change. Twenty minutes later, they were tooling along the road, a well-stocked basket under their feet.

"Tell me when I need to turn," said Adam, speaking for the first time since they had entered the road.

"It's not too far. I'm surprised you don't remember this place."

"I was only a boy the last time I visited Pixley with my father, and all I really recall is the hunting. When we came, we would hunt from morning to dusk," said Adam. "At that age, if it wasn't something I could catch, shoot, or ride, I took no notice of it—especially something like a folly."

"Not just a folly," she said with a trill of laughter. "But I suppose no one dared to call it by its name—not to your face anyway."

"The Fox's Folly? I should think not, though I would probably have agreed with them. What is the point in building something new and trying to make it look old?" asked Adam, glancing sideways at his passenger and smiling.

Grace returned his smile, finding herself comparing

the openness of his handsome face with his brother's studied charm. In her opinion, there was no contest.

"I think it is meant to be intriguing, finding the ruins of a Greek temple in the middle of the English countryside. Just beyond that stand of trees, that's the pathway."

He turned off the lane and drove a short way before the path dwindled and disappeared.

"You can leave the curricle here in the meadow," said Grace, her heart skipping a beat as he descended and circled the curricle to take her hand. Their gloved hands touched, and she felt a great impatience that the fine leather stood between them. Hopping lightly to the ground, he held her hands in his, their eyes meeting briefly before glancing away shyly.

Biting at her lower lip, Grace said huskily, "We'll have to climb to the top of the hill. The temple is just on the other side. It is really quite pretty. It overlooks the stream and a small valley," she added informatively as he removed the harness and hobbled Caesar.

Picking up the basket with one hand, he offered her his arm for the short climb. The going was rocky, and he was soon holding her hand as they climbed to the top of the rise.

"There, you see. It's really quite a good vista, don't you think?" she said, her eyes on him instead of the view. Reluctantly, she dragged her eyes away.

"Very picturesque," he replied, gazing down across the valley, with its grazing sheep and meandering stream. Adam turned to look at the young woman by his side, and his admiration for nature doubled. In the past, perhaps he had seen others, danced with others, whose beauty was more sublime, but at that moment, he thought he had never seen anything to compare with her beauty and grace.

Feeling his gaze, she glanced up at him and smiled. "There is the Fox's Folly," she said, pointing to his left.

Dragging his attention toward the direction indicated, he observed, "Good heavens, Father really went all-out, didn't he? I could almost believe it is a mound of ruins."

Without a moment's hesitation, Grace took his hand and led the way to the temple. "You see, there are the columns still standing and then these are the ones that have supposedly fallen. Wasn't it fortuitous that they fell into a sort of circle and that this big, flat stone landed on top of them, forming a perfect table for our picnic?" she said with a gurgle of laughter.

"Absolutely incredible, I should say," replied Adam, setting the basket down on the flat stone and reluctantly releasing her hand.

"I daresay Cook has put a tablecloth in there as well as blankets to cover our benches," said Grace, opening the basket and pulling out the linens, just as she predicted.

"Only one blanket," said Adam. "We shall have to share." He spread the wool cover over one of the fallen columns while Grace began unpacking their luncheon.

"Hm, chicken and ham, boiled eggs, a few meat pasties, several apples, and one pear, some new potatoes and little onions, and a box of Cook's wonderful little cakes. Just like her biscuits, they melt in your mouth."

"Then let us start with the cakes," said Adam, his mood light and frivolous.

The autumn sun shone brightly, and the sky was so blue the wispy clouds stood out in dazzling contrast. The air was clean and crisp, like an apple chilled in the cellar. Adam wished he could stay there forever, chatting over inconsequential matters so that he could listen to her throaty laugh, her velvety tones floating over him like a caress. He knew it was an afternoon he would never forget.

As they ate the simple repast, their conversation drifted from literature to music, and Adam asked about each girl at the school, mentioning the piece each one had played that morning. He was terrible with names, he confessed, but his powers of observation were such that Grace knew immediately which girl he was asking about.

"I can't believe you remember all the girls," she said finally as she replaced the flatware and plates in the basket.

"I just wish I were as good with names as I am with faces. It gets me in a great deal of trouble," he confessed, adding, "I still blush when I recall mistaking you for Mrs. Odstock."

"Oh, please do not put it like that—as if you couldn't tell us apart," said Grace.

Adam chuckled and shook his head, "I would never say such a daft thing. But it was embarrassing and could have been avoided if I had only remembered your name and the name Mrs. Lambert mentioned when she told me about my new housekeeper."

"I admit I was a bit puzzled, but I laughed about it later."

"I'm glad you could do so, but it is a shortcoming that has gotten me in trouble more than once. People expect better of the clergy."

"I don't see why they should expect you to be any different from other people," she said.

"That is because you are kind, Grace. I try, you know, but I don't think I'll ever change," he said with a sigh. "When I enter a large gathering, I often wish for someone by my side who could whisper names to me. I become so nervous, I swear I could forget my own brother."

The mention of the earl brought their easy camaraderie to an end, and Adam plucked up his courage to speak to Grace about his other concerns, starting with his mother's accusations about the impropriety of the girls learning to fence. The old awkwardness and formality reasserted itself immediately.

"Miss Edgewood, I hesitate to speak about this subject again; I know it upsets you."

"Then do not do so, Mr. Havenhurst. We must agree to disagree on the subject of the girls learning to swim."

"Rest assured that that is not what I wished to talk to you about. You have completely unmanned me on that subject," he replied, giving her a rueful grin. Then he sobered and continued. "I have another concern, I'm afraid."

"And what is that? If you are going to speak to me about the girls learning Latin or Greek, then pray do not."

"No, no, miss, uh . . ."

"Edgewood," she supplied, flashing him an impish grin.

"I didn't forget," he said, shaking his finger at her. "No, I see nothing morally wrong with any of those subjects, I assure you. Oh, I am not convinced of the necessity of teaching such subjects to girls, but there can be nothing wrong with it. No, it is something else, something which I may have misheard."

"Fencing," said Grace, turning to face him, her eyes lighting with amusement. Her expression did nothing to soothe the vicar's discomfort.

"Yes, fencing. Surely you can see the impropriety in teaching young ladies to fence, an occupation associated with war and violence."

"Mr. Havenhurst," she began with a little laugh, "you really must try to find some other task to occupy your time. Trying to reform me is hardly worth your trouble."

"I'm not . . . very well, perhaps I am trying to reform you, Miss Edgewood, but since I appear to be having little or no success, I don't see that we should, if you will excuse the pun, cross swords over this," said Adam, relieved that they could find a source of humor in this discussion. Perhaps this time, he would meet with more success.

Grace laughed, and said affably, "I am not trying to turn the girls into fencing masters, Mr. Havenhurst; it is merely another healthy activity that will encourage the girls to remain physically fit. And, I might add, other schools for young ladies do the same; fencing fosters grace, a highly useful attribute on the dance floor. Surely there is no harm in that," she added, placing her hand on his sleeve and smiling at him.

Adam was moved to return that smile, and shook his head. "I suppose there is no harm in it. But surely, girls are not as competitive as boys. I daresay they will not even enjoy fencing."

"You might be surprised, Mr. Havenhurst. I was always very competitive with my brothers. They were very condescending to me, of course, and that only led me to strive all the harder to beat them at whatever game we were playing."

"But you are speaking of the younger girls, surely."

"You know very little about girls, don't you? All of the girls will have the opportunity to learn the sport, if they wish, though I shan't force them."

"You know, Miss Edgewood, I have never known another lady like you," said Adam, placing his hand on top of hers. Then he cleared his throat and removed his hand.

He rose. Looking down at her, his manner changed again as he resumed his clerical role. "Have you considered what the girls will wear? They cannot possibly wear dresses."

"Of course not. Mrs. Brough has already made up a quantity of breeches and shirts," she said.

"Really, Miss Edgewood, it is not proper . . ."

Her eyes beseeched him, and she reached up, again touching his sleeve. Adam looked away for a moment, torn by his own desires.

He smiled hopefully as an idea struck him, and he asked, "Perhaps they could practice indoors?"

Grace shook her head glumly. "There is not enough room, without moving out furniture every time. What if they only practice in the stable yard, behind the house? Would that soothe your wounded sensibilities?" she said, unable to resist teasing him a little.

"Very well," he said, taking her hand to help her rise.

He held it a little too long, and Grace colored up at the warmth of his regard and his touch. Again he cleared his throat and dropped her hand.

As they strolled down the hill to the curricle, Adam risked their new harmony by bringing up one last dangerous topic—his brother. Immediately, he felt Grace stiffen.

"I don't wish to speak ill of my own brother, and he is a capital fellow in most regards, but he is . . . that is . . . I . . ."

"He is a rake, a man with a dangerous reputation," supplied Grace.

"Precisely, Miss Edgewood. I know you have your uncle to protect you, but I feel, in my position as your spiritual caretaker . . ."

"My what?" she asked, losing her struggle with laughter.

"Your spiritual . . . your vicar. At any rate, I feel I should warn you that it is perhaps unwise to spend so much time in Alex's company. I mean, you only drove out with him yesterday, and already the people of the village are speculating."

Her laughter disappeared, replaced by a deepening scowl. "And what are they speculating, Mr. Havenhurst?"

"I'm sure I don't know. I do not indulge in gossip."

"Really? Then how do you know that they are speculating?" she demanded.

"If you must know, Mrs. Odstock . . ."

"Mrs. Odstock? You will listen to your malicious housekeeper's gossip, but you say you do not gossip? You are a hypocrite, Mr. Havenhurst." She dropped his arm and turned to face him, her eyes blazing.

"It is not hypocritical to care for your good name, Miss Edgewood," he said, "and I think you should have a care for it, too. We may not like it, but the people of the village . . ."

"Have nothing to say to the matter. This is not London, where the latest *on-dit* is the bread and butter of the *ton*. I shall do as I please until the villagers start placing wagers on my virtue, like the so-called gentlemen at the clubs in London do, guessing how long it will be before I succumb to his charms."

Adam shook his head, unable to answer this attack. If he had not taken part in such wagers during his salad days, perhaps he could have expressed his outrage over her outrageous speech. But then he would truly have felt a hypocrite. He remained silent as she turned on her heel, marching rapidly toward the curricle.

Following more slowly, Adam reached the curricle after she had climbed in, not bothering to wait for his help. In the icy silence, he placed the basket on the floor of the curricle and set about harnessing Caesar. Climbing in beside her, Adam glanced at her stony profile. Grace was still fuming, but she hadn't given him the promise he wanted to hear, and Adam felt compelled to continue.

"Will you promise me, Miss Edgewood, to at least consider the fact that I may know more about this, about my brother, than you do?"

She lifted her chin and turned her head away.

"I have only your best interest at heart. I do not want to see you hurt," he pleaded.

Narrowing her eyes as she turned to face him, Grace snapped, "Did it ever occur to you, Mr. Havenhurst, that

I might enjoy your brother's company, that I do not give a fig that he is a rake, and that I absolutely delight in hearing his fulsome compliments?"

His eyes flashed, but Adam said nothing, and Grace continued furiously. "I can tell you one thing, Adam Havenhurst, it is a great deal more pleasant being with Alex than being with you and having to endure your constant scolding! If he steals a kiss or two, then it is well worth it! Now, take me home! I should have known better than to drive anywhere with you!"

Adam had never wanted so badly to shake a woman, and his reaction astonished him. His jaw clenched and unclenched; his fists did the same. He would not harm a hair on her head, of course. He was a gentleman, first and foremost. But he simply had to do something. She had challenged him as surely as if she had slapped his cheek with a white glove.

"You, Miss Edgewood, are a harridan and a hussy."

With this, he grabbed her and kissed her thoroughly, his lips taking possession of her mouth while his arms pulled her shapely breast against his hard chest. Time stood still, and then she was kissing him, her hands twined in his copper hair and her mouth opening at the gentle pressure of his tongue.

As suddenly as it began, Adam set her away from him. Gasping like a drowning man, he picked up the ribbons and gave Caesar the office to start. He was thoroughly shocked—shocked at his own behavior, to be sure, but more shocked at her passionate reaction. Surely, if she were a lady, she would have reacted differently! She should have slapped his face!

After a few yards, he stopped the curricle again. Without turning to face her, he said tightly, "Perhaps I was wrong about you and my brother, Miss Edgewood. I believe you are cut from the same cloth and should suit extremely well."

Not another word was said all the way back to Dodwell's Progressive Academy for Young Ladies. When they drove to the front door, the groom was nowhere to be seen, and Grace jumped to the ground unassisted. She hurried up the front steps without a backward glance.

The ribbons felt like lead in his hands as Adam lifted them to send Caesar on his way back to the little vicarage. He told himself he had been bewitched, that Grace Edgewood was a wanton, a strumpet.

But her lips on his had been so innocent, so sweet and unschooled, until she had abandoned herself in his arms. He wanted to turn the curricle around, to beg for her forgiveness.

He wanted to kiss her again.

Adam gritted his teeth. He was the vicar, and vicars did not go about kissing young ladies to whom they were not betrothed. He had treated her abominably, and he would have to write her a formal letter of apology. She would probably burn it without even opening it. He deserved no better.

"Stop it," he growled loudly, making Caesar's ear twitch back in his direction. "She was every bit as much at fault as I was. No one forced her to respond like she did. Undoubtedly, I have been right all along. Miss Edgewood is no better than she ought to be."

The sound of his words was like a death knell, chilling his heart to the very core. In a daze of confusion, Adam marveled that the light had gone out of the countryside.

It was only two o'clock.

Eight

Grace headed straight for the solitude of her room, but it was not to be. As she passed her uncle's library, Mrs. Stiles called, "Grace, won't you come here a moment?"

"I really would like to wash my face first," she lied.

"Oh, I think that can wait a moment," said her smiling friend. "Come and see what has arrived for you."

Grace retraced her steps and entered her uncle's library.

"It's all a hum, my girl. I don't know why Mrs. Stiles will get so excited about a little box," said Uncle Rhodes.

"It is precisely because it is a little box, Mr. Dodwell. A box just the right size for a piece of jewelry." Margaret placed a small box in Grace's hands and urged, "Open it."

It was tied with a red ribbon, and Grace carefully undid the bow, slipping the band off one end. Opening the box, she expelled her pent-up breath in admiration of the pearl necklace with a pear-shaped emerald set in gold in the center.

"Oh, I cannot accept this."

"Who is it from?" asked her uncle.

"From the Earl of Foxworth, of course," said Mrs. Stiles, impatient to have this fact certified. "Open the card."

Grace read the short missive out loud. " 'To thank you for your care and attention of my wards, and in admiration. Your servant, Foxworth.' "

"How lovely," said Mrs. Stiles with a sigh.

"I don't know, Mrs. Stiles. It seems a bit extravagant, don't you think, Grace?" said her uncle, taking the necklace and holding the emerald up to the lamp. "This is the real thing, not paste."

"Should I send it back to him?" she asked.

"Well, you wouldn't want anyone to get the wrong idea, and people are bound to talk when they see you wearing a new necklace. Perhaps you should ask the vicar for his opinion," said Margaret Stiles.

"I will do no such thing. Besides which, people always do talk, and we should take no notice of them," said Grace, thinking of Adam's comments about her driving out with his brother.

She took the necklace from her uncle and crossed the room to the gilt-framed mirror over the fireplace, admiring the effect against her skin in it. It matched her eyes perfectly, and perhaps its green fire would stoke the flames of Adam's jealousy.

"It is lovely, and I see nothing wrong in a gift given in gratitude."

"If you say so, my dear," said her uncle, returning to his book.

"You should wear it to services tomorrow. It will look lovely with that green silk gown."

"Yes, Margaret, I was thinking the same thing," said Grace, a mischievous grin playing on her lips.

She wanted to think that the vicar's lecture about his rakish brother had been fueled by jealousy, but she couldn't be certain. The necklace would prove once and for all if she had a chance of awakening Adam's passion.

* * *

"What the devil do you want?" Adam demanded when he arrived home and spied his brother sprawled on the only decent chair in his parlor.

"A nice, pleasant way to greet your favorite brother," drawled the earl, not bothering to rise. He took a deep drink of his brandy, all the while watching Adam over the rim of the glass.

"You are my only brother, so I have little choice," said Adam, pulling a hard Windsor chair closer to the fireplace and warming his hands to the fire. The afternoon had turned decidedly chilly, he thought, as he scowled at his brother.

"What is it you want, Alex? I'm in no mood to banter words with you this afternoon."

"So I see," said Alex. Sitting up straight and leaning toward his younger brother, he thumped Adam's chest, and added, "Very well, then I will get to the point straightaway. It concerns Miss Edgewood."

"What about her?" asked Adam warily.

"You know I have had my eye on her. She's quite a beauty, and that figure of hers is . . . well." The earl grinned and expelled a short whistle, using his hands to paint a voluptuous figure in the air.

"There is no need to be vulgar. Just get on with it."

"Very well, I have sent a gift around to her—you know, one of the usual necklaces like I have made up for . . ."

"Yes, yes, I know. Go on," snapped Adam, grasping the edge of his chair to keep from strangling his brother.

"I am wondering if, when she accepts it—and me," he added with a lurid grin, "should I take her back to London with me, or merely carry on here? I mean, people in the country are not as accepting of these little arrangements as London is, and it will be the devil . . . what the deuce . . . by Jove, Adam, I'll . . ."

Adam grabbed his brother's neck, pinning it under his

arm, and dragged him to the front door. When he had finished shoving him outside, he leaned against the frame, panting, his dark eyes black with rage.

From his vantage point on the ground, Alex said, "What the devil was that about?"

"If you don't know . . ."

The earl clambered to his feet, dusting off his coat and breeches as he continued. "I was just trying to get a second point of view on the situation, blast you, and I figured you were the only person around here who was reasonable enough to have a discussion about it. I take it, however, that you think London would be . . ."

"You're wasting your breath, Alex. What you're going to do or not do, where you're going to go or not go, just save it for Miss Edgewood because I don't give a damn!"

Alex's shout of laughter only served to enrage Adam more, and he rushed forward, head down, to butt his brother in the stomach. Caught off guard, the earl went flying, with Adam falling on top of him, his fist drawn back.

From the road where he had stopped his horse, Mr. Gray, the blacksmith, called, "I say, Vicar, is that a part of a new plan to win people to your flock?"

The earl shoved Adam off his chest and scrambled to his feet. He leaned down and offered his hand to his brother. Adam glared at him, and Alex cocked his head toward the newcomer in warning. Reluctantly, Adam accepted his help.

"Just having a bit of a brotherly discussion, sir. I'm afraid boys will be boys," said the earl, clapping Adam on the back and whispering under his breath, "Smile, you dolt."

Adam forced a tight little smile to his lips and nodded. "Just a bit of fun, Mr. Gray," he said.

"I know how it goes. I have a brother, too," said the

blacksmith, climbing down from his broad-backed mount.

"What brings you out this way, Mr. Gray?"

"Mrs. Odstock said that chimney on her stove was not pulling right. I told her I would have a look at it this afternoon."

"Oh, good. Just go right on in," said Adam.

The big man wagged a finger at the two brothers and said, "If you two can behave."

"Ha, ha, good one, Mr. Gray," said Adam, watching until the blacksmith disappeared into the house. Then, glaring at his brother, he said a terse, "Good day to you, Alex."

"Adam, I don't know what you're so upset about. It's not as if you wish to take up with Miss Edgewood yourself. I mean, I know some vicars have a bit of fluff on the side . . ." Looking up at his younger brother from the ground once again, Alex exclaimed, "Dash it, Adam! You do that one more time, and I'll . . ."

Adam responded by walking away.

"All you have to do is tell me, little brother, and I'll leave the field open for you."

"I don't need your leftovers," said Adam, wincing at the words. "I am only concerned with Grace's well-being. That's all there is to it."

"Grace. A pretty name for a pretty lady," said Alex, dusting off the back of his breeches, keeping a wary eye on Adam.

The earl shook his head as he watched his brother turn and go back into the house, shutting the door with a decided snap.

"You know, Adam," the earl said loudly, knowing his younger brother was still listening, "there's no need to get blue-deviled about it. She may return the necklace."

The earl listened for a moment, then untied his horse and mounted, whistling as he rode off.

Behind the closed door, Adam drove his fist against the wall, not even noticing the pain or the blood dripping from his knuckles. Nor did he notice the blacksmith, who was standing in the doorway of the kitchen.

After a moment, while Adam leaned his head against the wall, oblivious to everything but the emotional pain in his breast, Mr. Gray poked his head into the parlor and announced that he had mended the stove.

"I'll be going now," he said, edging past Adam and opening the front door.

Adam pulled himself together and walked to the opening.

"Send me the bill, Mr. Gray."

"There's no charge, Mr. Havenhurst. It was just a clog, and I'm happy to help. Good day," he said with a cheery wave as he rode back toward the village.

Adam grimaced. Before dark, the entire village would know about the fight with his brother. They would probably know about his—he looked down—his bloodied knuckles. They would also guess the cause.

The good vicar shook his head, shut the door, and poured another generous portion of brandy into the glass his brother had drained.

Adam knew Grace would never consent to becoming his brother's mistress; she was a lady. He hoped, however, she would only be angered and not disappointed by his brother's insult.

Alex hadn't always been a rake. His marriage to the delicate Lady Elaine Sparks had been a love match. When she died giving birth to Phillip, their second son, Alex had gone wild with grief. He had buried his wife and his reputation in a few short months.

In his younger days, Adam had tried to ape his older brother by conquering as many of the ladies as he could. It had been a game to him. He and his friends had delighted in the juicy *on-dits* about his brother's exploits and had tried to top each other, knowing they could never top their idol, the Earl of Foxworth. They had tried to win the favor of the Season's reigning belle, outdoing each other with outrageous compliments, flowers, and poetry. They had never considered the young ladies, had never wondered if their hopes had been shattered when their beaux callously turned away to fawn over the next Season's beauty.

The thought that Grace might be hurt when she realized his brother was offering, not marriage, but a carte blanche, was painful. The thought that she might be heartbroken was intolerable.

Adam drained the glass and poured another.

It was not the proper thing to do, of course, trying to make one man jealous by flaunting his brother's very expensive gift. Even Grace knew that much, but the next day she found herself looking forward to church services with a sense of satisfaction. Unladylike and childish, perhaps, but she took special care to make certain her golden curls were perfectly coifed and that her dark green gown showed off the pearl and emerald necklace to advantage.

In her reticule, Grace carried a note composed with great care, thanking the earl for his generous gift. The note would be hard to miss, written on pale blue vellum and scented with some rather strong perfume that had belonged to her mother, she thought, as the odor emanating from her reticule assailed her nostrils again. Grace looked down at her hands folded primly in her lap and smiled. She had been careful to keep the wording completely innocuous. The last thing she wanted was to encourage the earl, but Adam needn't know that!

She would hand his brother the note when Adam would be certain to see it. If she was lucky, between the gift of the necklace and the note, the priggish Mr. Havenhurst would be so jealous, he would be tempted to declare for her then and there.

"What are you so cheery about this morning, my dear?" asked her uncle from his perch on the rear-facing seat in the old traveling carriage.

"Why, nothing. I'm just happy the day has turned out fine. It is lovely this morning, is it not?" she asked, gazing out the window.

"She's up to something, Mrs. Stiles. Why else would it take her a full fifteen minutes more to get ready?" commented her uncle with a wink. "If you ask me, she's expecting more than an excellent sermon in the service this morning."

"Uncle Rhodes, I promise it is no such thing," said Grace, her twinkling eyes giving her away.

He chuckled and reached across to take her chin, turning it from left to right, and shaking his head. "I only hope this isn't going to cause a great hubbub, miss. It's a pretty bauble, but you may find it is not worth the trouble it may cause."

"Do not tease her so, Mr. Dodwell. After all, we told her it was quite proper for her to accept the gift."

"We did? I thought you told her so, but that is neither here nor there, my dear Mrs. Stiles. We must remember that our Grace is not one of our students. She is quite able to make her own decisions, and," he said, sniffing and wrinkling his nose, "unless I mistake the matter, she has made up her mind."

The carriage stopped, and the round man escaped before Grace could respond to his teasing. She allowed him to hand down Mrs. Stiles first, and then she descended, slowly, expectantly.

"Hurry, my dear, we are very late," said her uncle, stepping quickly toward the old stone church with a lady on each arm.

As they entered the dimly lit church, the vicar paused

only a second in his sermon. Quickly and quietly, they took their places in the pew in front of all their students. Grace glanced across the aisle and spied the earl. Seated in his high-backed pew, she was only able to see the tip of his nose. She leaned forward as far as she could to attract his attention, but her uncle tugged on her arm, pulling her back.

Glancing up, Grace turned crimson. Glaring down at her, oblivious to the rest of the congregation, was the vicar, her vicar. His eyes riveted on the large, winking emerald on her chest, he stammered, he blushed; finally, he managed to drag his eyes back to the text on the altar.

Grace bit her lower lip, suddenly unsure of her great plans. She looked at the ceiling and the walls, but her gaze came to rest on the earl, who paid no heed to the gaping parishioners behind them when he twisted in his seat, a wide smile on his handsome face as his eyes also became transfixed on her chest. If her wish had been granted at that moment, Grace would have melted onto her seat and ended as a mere puddle on the floor.

The quiet of the morning exploded. "It was St. Peter the apostle, who asked our Lord, 'How oft shall my brother sin against me, and I forgive him?' "

Eyes widened at the booming voice; Grace could almost feel the people rubbing their hands together in anticipation. They had not attended this service expecting a spectacle, but they were certainly being treated to one!

With a rustle of pages as he leafed quickly through his Bible, Adam continued, his compelling voice requiring the attention of all who were present—not that wild horses could have dragged any of them away!

"But how difficult it is, for we are not holy like our Lord. We may try to forgive our brother who sins against us, but are we strong enough? No! No! Therefore, my friends, I tell you, do not lead your brother astray by sinning against him. For as Saint Peter warns us, 'Abstain from fleshly lusts, which war against the soul.' Surely we can do no less than to take his advice."

Adam slammed the Bible closed and took his seat. Swallowing his laughter, Rhodes Dodwell opened his mouth and began singing, " 'How can we sinners know, our sins on earth forgiven. . . .' " Slowly the rest of the congregation joined in—except Grace, who was too mortified; Adam, who was too angry; and the Earl of Foxworth, who was hardly able to stand upright as he tried to contain his laughter.

When the song ended, everyone remained frozen for a few seconds, unsure how to proceed without guidance from the pulpit. Rhodes Dodwell turned to Patrick and issued concise instructions for seeing the students back to school. Then he turned his attention to his niece, who appeared to be stricken with paralysis. This action made the rest of the congregation spring to life.

In the scramble for a good vantage point after the service, Grace managed to evade them all, slipping out a side door with Mrs. Stiles, who wasn't quite certain what had happened, and her Uncle Rhodes. He was sent to fetch the carriage while Grace and Mrs. Stiles waited behind a clump of bushes.

A group of curious onlookers followed Uncle Rhodes back to their hiding place to witness their departure. Among them was Mrs. Odstock, who looked Grace up and down, nodding her head and rubbing her hands together.

"A rather ignominious exit, my dear," said her uncle as he helped her into the carriage.

"Not now, Mr. Dodwell," whispered Margaret Stiles, putting a bracing arm around her young friend's shoulders.

Stone-faced, Grace stared out the window, her eyes never focusing on the passing landscape or noticing the fine fall morning.

* * *

"You'll come to dinner, of course," said the dowager countess to her son as she left the church.

"I don't know, Mother," he replied, trying to move her along so the next person could shake his hand and stare at him with probing eyes. His mother, however, refused to move until she had the answer she wanted.

"Very well, Mother, I shall be there in an hour. Good-bye."

"Good-bye, my dear," she said, lifting her gloved hand for a kiss. When he had performed this, she moved away, leaving the field open for the earl, who grinned, shook his head, and followed the countess to his elegant carriage. The disappointed parishioners drifted away, leaving Adam alone.

Adam Havenhurst was not a great spiritualist. If he was devout in the performance of his duties, it resulted from a strong sense of habit and honor, rather than any deep religious beliefs. Having had little reason to beg for mercy in a life of excessive luxury, his prayers were more mechanical than heartfelt. But Adam was moved to prayer after seeing Grace, looking so breathtakingly beautiful, only to realize she was wearing the necklace that was akin to his brother's signature—the same pearl and emerald necklace he gave to all his mistresses.

He entered the quiet little church and turned, carefully closing the heavy oak door. Sitting down on one of the rough benches at the back of the church, he buried his face in his hands and prayed.

Rising, he realized he would find no peace in church this day; peace would be denied to him forever, until he put Grace Edgewood out of his mind—and heart—completely.

* * *

Grace put on a brave front for the girls when they returned to the school. She managed to smile brightly while they were watching. When she reached the privacy of her room, her mask slipped when she paused in front of the mirror and caught sight of the pearl and emerald necklace. Like a sail that dies along with the wind, she crumpled onto the velvet-upholstered stool in front of the dressing table.

What on earth had she been thinking, accepting such a gift from the Earl of Foxworth? She was not as green as all that, but in her desire to make the vicar jealous, she hadn't used good judgment.

Just as she was about to remove it, Mrs. Stiles scratched on the door and then entered, sitting down on a nearby chair. "My dear girl, I am so sorry."

"Never mind, Margaret. It was a foolish notion, trying to make the vicar jealous. I only succeeded in making him angry and making a fool of myself."

"Oh, it is not so bad as that," said her friend.

"Perhaps not, but I now realize I must give the necklace back to the earl. I certainly shan't wear it again," she said with a smile. "I mean, I may not be able to win the vicar's heart, but I have no desire to give him an apoplexy."

"Oh my, he was so angry," breathed Margaret, her eyes growing wide.

"He is a quick study, though; you must admit that," said Grace with a giggle. "I mean, to pull a verse out of his hat like that."

"It was perfect, really." Margaret laughed, adding in a deep voice, " 'How oft shall my brother sin against me?' "

This sent both ladies into whoops again, until Margaret gasped. "Oh, no, Grace, we mustn't, we really mustn't."

"You are quite right," said Grace, but the laughter was like a tonic, and she couldn't resist adding, "But then, when the vicar had gone, and without missing a beat, Uncle Rhodes broke into that song . . . I only wish I had not been so miserable and could have enjoyed it more."

They laughed and laughed, their good humor restored. When they finally sobered, Grace rose and hugged her friend.

"What was that for?" asked Margaret.

"For making me feel better," said Grace. "I shall have a great deal of explaining to do when I next see my vicar; I only hope I can make him understand."

"I'm sure you can, my dear. You know, I have been thinking about something you said the other night, when you wondered why we ladies cannot simply tell a man how we feel about them."

"Yes, it was foolish of me, but it would be so much easier than all these little games."

"I quite agree. As a matter of fact, I am wondering if perhaps I should try your suggestion."

Grace cocked her head to one side, her hand touching the necklace. "I don't know if you should follow my advice, Margaret. Only see where my ideas have led me."

"Oh, you'll come about. As for me? I have been here for two years; nothing has changed, nor is it likely to do so unless I stir things up a bit."

Grace knelt down beside Margaret's chair and took her hand, squeezing it gently.

"You know I wish you the best of luck, Margaret. I think it would be lovely to be able to call you Aunt. I only hope Uncle Rhodes has more sense than Mr. Havenhurst."

Margaret nodded and said, "Do not give up on your vicar yet, Grace. He'll get over this, you just wait and see."

Grace straightened and pulled her friend to her feet. "I hope you may be right. But for you, Mrs. Stiles, there is no time like the present," she said, kissing Margaret's soft cheek and sending her out the door. "Good luck."

"Thank you, dear. I need the luck and the courage."

Grace sank into the chair her friend had just vacated. She hoped her uncle would be sensible. She knew he was quite fond of Margaret, but he was an old bachelor, set in his ways. He might not like the idea of marriage, and anything less . . . well, Margaret wouldn't have it.

Ten minutes later, there was another knock on her door and a maid entered, asking her to step downstairs to her uncle's study. Hurrying along the corridor, Grace's heart thumped loudly in her breast.

Entering the room, she frowned, warned by Margaret's surreptitious finger to the lips. Grace gave a quick nod to signal that she understood.

Smiling at her uncle, she asked, "You wanted to see me, Uncle Rhodes?"

"Yes, my dear. Do sit down. Mrs. Stiles and I have been tossing around a few ideas about this fencing thing."

With a quick glance at her friend, Grace murmured, "Yes?"

"Now, I do not wish to denigrate your teaching ability on this score, but do you not think it would be wise, at least at first, to have someone with a little more experience come and teach the subject? I thought of one of your brothers, but Mrs. Stiles suggested we ask the Earl of Foxworth."

Grace groaned at that name and shook her head vehemently.

"I know, Margaret, that you meant well, but Foxworth is the last man I would ask to help us."

"But my dear, your plan . . . ?"

Rhodes Dodwell looked from one lady to the other and back again. "What plan is this, Grace?"

"A very ill-conceived plan, Uncle, which is no longer

in operation." She flashed Margaret a warning glance and added, "I will send for David immediately. James would be a great help, too, but since he is recently betrothed—unlike other people I could mention," she said, with a significant look at her friend, "I daresay James will not wish to leave home at the moment. Still, I will mention it to David. Having two expert instructors would not come amiss."

"Excellent, my dear," said her uncle, returning to his newspaper, which was spread all over his desk.

"Margaret, may I have a word with you?" asked Grace.

"Certainly, dear," said the older woman, following her out the door.

"What happened?" asked Grace as soon as she had closed the door to the study.

"I . . . I just couldn't, my dear," said Margaret, tears springing to her pale eyes.

"Never mind," said Grace, placing a bracing arm around her friend's plump shoulders. "It was probably a very bad idea anyway."

"Where is Alex, Mother? I want a word with him," said Adam as he joined his mother at Foxworth Manor.

"Heavens, I don't know where Foxworth has gone. I can never keep up with him, as well you know. You are the only one who is always so assiduous in your duty to your mother. Foxworth never thinks to tell me he is going out, much less does he indulge me with his destination. I vow, were it not for you, my dear, I . . ."

Her words blurred as Adam's attention wandered. He had heard it all before and didn't need to listen anymore. He could recite his mother's diatribes by heart, if needed. Alex had not been lying when he said he was grateful that Adam had been born. Sometimes, Adam felt he had been born merely as a sounding board for his mother's many complaints.

Today, however, he had other things to occupy his mind. He knew where his brother had gone. Since Grace had accepted Alex's necklace, his brother would be flying to her side, sweeping her off her feet—quite literally. The vision of Alex and Grace in a passionate embrace rose before his eyes and he leapt to his feet, startling his mother into momentary silence.

"Excuse me, Mother, I have suddenly remembered a previous engagement. You will forgive me, I know, but duty calls, and I must obey." Without giving her a chance to protest, Adam hurried out of the room, down the hall, and out the back door to fetch Caesar from the stables.

The groom, who had not yet removed the harness, threw him the ribbons, and he drove away at a smart pace.

Adam had not covered more than a mile when the rain began. It was gentle and warm at first; then the wind began to howl and the rain came in sheets, stinging his face as he urged Caesar ever faster. Suddenly, the curricle tilted wildly, and he watched the left wheel go spinning off the road and into the ditch. Through skillful handling, Adam managed to bring Caesar to a stop without ending up in a heap in the middle of the road.

After unharnessing the big horse, Adam pushed the lopsided curricle to the side of the road. Then he scrambled up on Caesar's back and turned him toward the vicarage.

To the devil with his brother and Miss Edgewood. A sneeze shook his body. They deserved each other!

"How nice of you to call, my lord," said Mrs. Stiles, opening the door to the parlor so that he could enter.

"It is my pleasure, Mrs. Stiles," replied the earl, blinking as he surveyed the room and realized he was not going to be granted a private interview with Miss Edgewood. All the girls, young and old, were sitting in the middle of the room. Someone began playing the pianoforte, and the girls rose, performing some sort of ritual dance around the chairs before the music stopped and they scuttled onto the chairs once more amid giggles and squeals.

"Just excuse me for a moment, my lord. I'll relieve Grace at the pianoforte, and you and she can have a comfortable coze," said Mrs. Stiles.

A closer survey of the far corner of the parlor revealed Mr. Dodwell slumbering on a blue-striped sofa. The earl's two wards were among the numbers playing the strange musical game, and they contented themselves by waving at him.

The music started again, as did the circular procession. His attention was caught by Miss Edgewood, who was walking toward him, her face a little pink, but smiling. He was relieved that the scene in church hadn't made her missish.

Bowing over her hand, the earl kept possession of it, leading her toward the door. Grace held back, shaking her head.

"I appreciate your wanting to stay and play the game, my dear Miss Edgewood, but I really would appreciate the opportunity to speak with you in private," said the earl, favoring her with an intimate smile.

Grace hesitated, her hand sliding unthinkingly to the necklace she still wore.

The music stopped again, and the scrambling recommenced. Abigail and Olivia squealed as they tried to take the same chair. Grace turned to watch, finally going forward and removing the chair and both girls. After a few quiet words with the two feuding girls, she returned to the earl. Looking over her shoulder, she raised one brow in warning to the girls, who continued to squabble.

The earl gave her hand a little tug, and Grace followed him out of the room and down the hall to her uncle's private study.

He saw her seated on the leather sofa and sat down beside her, his thigh touching hers. She wished suddenly that the green silk gown were made of sturdier stuff.

"This necklace could not have found a more beautiful setting," he said, touching the emerald that rested against her white breast. His fingertips fluttered across her skin, coming to rest on her shoulder. He leaned closer, and Grace ducked her head. The earl, however, was not to be denied. Turning to face her, he lifted her chin and placed a gentle kiss on her mouth. Drawing back, he smiled down at her, expecting a blush and a simper.

Instead, he received a powerful blow to his stomach that sent him sprawling against the arm of the sofa. Sputtering, he demanded, "What the devil was that for?"

"What do you think it was for, my lord?" exclaimed Grace, rising and standing toe to toe with him, her eyes blazing and her chin thrust out defiantly.

"So you are upset with me about this morning," he said, a half smile replacing his bewildered frown.

"Why the devil should *I* be upset with *you* about this morning?" she demanded, her voice dripping with disdain.

The earl's smile grew, and Grace couldn't help but return it. He was quite a good sport, smiling when she had just punched him in the breadbasket.

"I thought you might be angry that I turned around and stared at you, causing a scene," he said. "I confess I shouldn't have, but I couldn't help myself, and the treat of seeing you, wearing my necklace, was worth all the trouble, and more."

"Stuff and nonsense! If I hadn't been so stupid and

worn this necklace . . ." she said, reaching behind her neck and struggling with the clasp. She shivered when he reached around her neck and unfastened it.

"Then perhaps there is still hope for me?" he said softly, holding out his hand to return the necklace to her. "This little bauble was meant to bring us closer, much closer, not to come between us. When I saw you wearing it, I thought you understood my offer."

Grace put her hands behind her back and stepped away, shaking her head. "Offer? Not an offer of marriage?" The earl shook his head and Grace added, "I see. Well, it seems we have been at cross purposes, my lord."

"Cross purposes?"

"Yes, I accepted the necklace as a gift, my lord. As you said in your note, a gift of gratitude. I know I shouldn't have; it was too expensive and quite improper."

"Surely we needn't adhere to Society's narrow rules," he said, taking a step closer.

"Yes, we must; I must. It was naive of me to accept it; I would never have done so, had I known it was a . . . payment," she added quietly, hanging her head in shame. How could she have been so very gullible?

Again he lifted her chin, but this time, he did not attempt to kiss her. After studying her for a moment, the earl dropped his hand and turned away, striding toward the door.

Pausing, he glanced back at her, a reflective light in his eyes. "I apologize if I gave you the wrong impression." Grace only shook her head, and he added thoughtfully, "Perhaps you would be worth it. Only time will tell."

With this cryptic comment, he was gone, and Grace sank onto the leather sofa again, her breath catching as she began to sob.

After a few minutes, she forced herself to stop crying. Taking out her handkerchief, she dabbed at her splotchy face. When had she given herself license to be a watering pot? she thought.

Moving to the mirror over the fireplace, she studied her reflection. It would never do; everyone would know she had been crying. How silly of her to shed tears over the earl; she didn't care anything about him. What did it matter to her if he had gotten the wrong idea about her because she had accepted his extravagant gift?

The tears started to flow again, and Grace knew she couldn't deny the real reason for the tears. Had it been Adam stealing a kiss, she would have welcomed it. As a matter of fact, he would have had a difficult time of it, getting away from her. A watery smile greeted her in the mirror.

Adam was tired, wet, and frustrated by the time he reached the vicarage. After seeing to Caesar, he entered the house, threw off his wet clothes, donned his dressing gown, and poured himself a glass of brandy. Tossing it down quickly, he picked up the bottle and adjourned to the tiny parlor, planning to get very drunk.

An hour later, he called "Come in" when someone knocked on the door, but he didn't attempt to rise. He was glad he hadn't bothered when he discerned it was only his brother.

"Devil take me, I believe the good vicar is castaway," said the earl, strolling into the room and perching on the only other chair.

Lurching forward in his seat, Adam glared at his brother. "Not castaway, merely foxed," he said, congratulating himself on not slurring his words. "So, is it done? Are you taking her back to London with you?"

"You know, old man, I may have to plant you a facer when you are sober," replied the earl, reaching for the bottle and glass. He poured a full measure and swallowed it in a gulp.

"You could try," said Adam with sudden sharpness. Then he leaned back in the chair, running a hand through his copper locks and shaking his head to clear it. The action had the opposite effect, and he had to close his eyes to keep the room from spinning.

"So what did the eccentric Miss Edgewood say when you offered her carte blanche? I suppose she leapt at the chance to be with an earl, to go to London."

"Why don't you shut your mouth, Adam? You're drunk, and you're being insulting, both to me and to Miss Edgewood."

Angry, Adam took the bottle back and turned it up, taking a short swallow that burned its way down his throat, sobering him in a way nothing else could.

"So what did happen, Alex?" he asked, wiping a dribble of brandy from his chin with his sleeve, just like a little boy.

"It didn't go as I planned. First, I kissed her."

Adam's stomach tightened.

"And then she punched me so hard in the stomach that I almost fell off the sofa," he added with an admiring chuckle.

"She hit you?" asked Adam, his heart lightening.

"Harder than you could," said his brother, rubbing his stomach at the memory. "Then she gave me back the necklace."

"She gave you back the necklace? Well, that must be a first," said Adam with a drunken giggle that earned him a hostile scowl.

"So now what are you going to do? Take Mother and leave Pixley? I mean, you wouldn't want to stay here now," said Adam hopefully, "having been bested by a girl."

Alex didn't respond to his taunt, only saying thoughtfully, "No, I'm not ready to go back to London. There are too many attractions around here. I haven't given up on Miss Edgewood yet. I don't know, maybe I rushed my fences with her." He glanced at Adam, but he failed to notice the dangerous glint in his brother's eyes, and he continued. "What do you think? I mean, you know her better than I do; perhaps you can tell me something to help me persuade her about the advantages of accepting my protection."

"Why, you bloody bas—!" growled Adam, swinging wildly and catching his brother with a right cross to the eye that sent him sprawling. Standing over his brother, nursing his raw knuckles, Adam added fiercely, "I ought to tear you limb from limb."

One hand covering his injured eye, the earl leapt to his feet, ready to do battle. Adam lunged for him, missed, and lost his balance, ending up on the floor, flat on his face.

With a rumble of satisfied laughter, Alex squatted on his heels and grabbed his brother's hair, lifting his head roughly.

"As I said a minute ago, Adam, when you're sober, I'm going to plant you a facer. We'll talk more in a few days when you can stand up straight. In the meanwhile, I'm leaving. I won't be able to see a thing out of this eye in an hour."

"Good," mumbled Adam, rolling over and glaring up at his brother.

"I don't know what your problem is with me and Grace, but I haven't given up on her; she may just be playing for higher stakes. With most women, I can tell, but Grace is different."

"Higher stakes?" murmured Adam.

Rubbing his stomach at the remembrance of her punch and grimacing, the earl continued, "Yes, you know— marriage. She's not the first, but she'll catch cold at that game. I mean, what do I want with another wife? Elaine was . . . well, I might not be so lucky a second time. It's not as if I need an heir, not with the two boys. Still, these negotiations can be dangerous; your Miss Edgewood packs quite a powerful punch."

"I hope she uses a gun the next time," Adam snarled.

The earl shook his head, chuckling as he added, "There is something about her though. Perhaps she would keep me from being bored. Who knows, maybe I ought to just marry the chit."

With this, the earl departed.

Adam struggled to rise, lost his balance again, and found relief in blessed oblivion.

Despair was not an emotion the Honorable Adam Havenhurst had ever indulged in, and the bleak situation he now found himself in was not going to win and make him begin. He awoke before dawn on Monday morning with his head throbbing and only a dim recollection of what had happened between him and his brother the day before. The cottage was dark and icy cold, proof that autumn had finally arrived to stay.

Adam built a fire in the kitchen, put the kettle on, and sat down at the table, holding his aching head in his hands. The chill he had contracted the previous day was trying to take hold, and when he sneezed, stars burst forth in front of his eyes.

As he saw it, he had two things to do this day, one of which might change his life forever. First, he had to apologize to his brother for attacking him; Alex didn't deserve an apology, perhaps, but a vicar ought to be a man of peace. So, as distasteful as it might be, he would ride over to Foxworth Manor and offer his apology—and try very hard to resist the temptation to draw his brother's cork again.

Then, he would go to see Grace—Miss Edgewood, he corrected, shaking his head and again unleashing that devilish earthquake pounding in his head. He closed his eyes and remained very still until the throbbing subsided.

This time, he vowed, he would not berate her at all or attempt to instruct her on any subject. Instead, he would . . .

Oh, the devil take him, he didn't know what he should do. He could not allow her to accept his brother's offer. What could he possibly say that would prevent her from doing so? he thought, wracking his foggy mind for a solution.

What would keep Grace . . . well, there was one thing that might work. He could always offer for her himself— not a slip on the shoulder, but marriage.

Not considering how his action would affect his aching head, the vicar sat bolt upright, his eyes wide with amazement. He ignored the throbbing at his temples while he explored this remarkable notion.

"You've lost what little sense you ever possessed," he muttered to himself. "Marry the girl? She barely tolerates you!"

Adam rose and poured himself a cup of boiling water. While he went through the mechanical motions of making his tea, his mind was working at a feverish pace. He came up with a dozen reasons why he should not offer for Grace, but he could conceive of only one reason why he should—he was quite thoroughly besotted with the chit. The idea made him wince.

How could such a thing have happened? How could he, a vicar, fall in love with a girl who was the antithesis of what a vicar's wife should be? If he were to marry her, she would keep his household, not to mention his entire parish, in a constant state of turbulence. He clenched his jaw, scowling as he envisioned his life, wed to such a strong, earthy creature. He would be forever smoothing over her faux pas with his parishioners or soothing her ruffled feathers.

Adam took another sip of the strong tea and closed his eyes; suddenly, she was there, in the tiny kitchen with him, bending over the oven, leaning over his shoulder. He could almost smell that sweet scent of lavender as her curls tickled his cheek.

Adam groaned, but this time it was not from the pain in his head; its source was deeper and infinitely more powerful.

What if she didn't accept? What if she didn't love him?

The idea was intolerable, he thought. Somehow, he would make her love him, make her see that she was meant to be here, in this poky little kitchen, loving him. Oh, it wouldn't be easy convincing her, but he recalled the taste of her sweet lips on his—a memory he had relegated to the dark recesses of his mind; it bolstered his confidence, making his hopes a reality.

Adam looked about the empty kitchen and smiled. He allowed himself the luxury of again imagining her there, fixing his tea, laughing as he shared some story about his work. A mistress for the little vicarage, that was what was missing from the ramshackle house. A wife for him, to fill his ramshackle life, he thought, his smile widening.

He looked about him, plans for enlarging the place swimming in his mind. They would need to have a proper sitting room, and a bigger bedroom. He grinned, but would not allow himself to think about Grace in conjunction with the bedroom—or the bed. They would need other rooms, too. Another bedroom for the nursery, and a place for a couple of servants, a maid for her, and a nanny for. . . .

The picture he was painting would have to wait. First, he would have to ask her to be his wife. What was that silly, formal phrase a fellow was supposed to utter? Ah yes, he should ask her to make him the happiest of men.

Adam grinned; considering their constant brangling, it was an unlikely phrase, but it was the truth. If Grace would consent to being his wife, he would be the happiest of men.

Afterward, she could cause no end of trouble with his parishioners, could argue with him from morning to night, just as long as she was there to share his life.

Yes, they would have a time of it; they both had tempers. He would be forever soothing her ruffled feathers over this or that.

But oh, what fun that would be, soothing those beautiful, wonderful feathers. . . .

Nine

Grace went down to the kitchen to consult with Cook about the week's menus and to warn her that their numbers would be increasing. Cook, who had also served Grace's mother, was delighted to hear that the "boys" would be paying them a visit, and she set about adding all their favorites to the menus.

With this accomplished, Grace decided a stroll in the garden would help her clear her thoughts before holding class. The morning was chilly, and she pulled her thick woolen shawl about her shoulders.

She had spent the previous evening in a fog of confusion and self-contempt. While she might excuse her own naiveté where the earl was concerned, she could not forgive herself for giving Adam a disgust of her by wearing the necklace. Her plan to make him jealous had gone terribly awry. She would be lucky if he ever addressed another civil word to her.

On this demoralizing note, the tears welled in her green eyes, and she took out her handkerchief.

"What is it? Tears on such a fine day?"

Grace whirled around, a broad smile on her face as she was caught up in her brother's beefy arms.

"James! I'm so delighted you could come, too," she exclaimed, standing on tiptoe to kiss his cheek.

"What about me?" asked her other giant of a brother,

pulling her against his broad chest and squeezing her tightly.

"And you, too, David. How I've missed you!" she declared.

Smiling up at one and then the other, her bravado crumbled and she astounded her brothers by bursting into tears.

On the way to Foxworth Manor, Adam stopped by the blacksmith's and arranged to have his curricle hauled in and repaired. Next, he rode straight to the manor, where his brother's trusted valet informed him stiffly that his lordship would be unavailable for the next week, at the very least, until he had recovered from his blackened eye. This was delivered with such a sigh of wounded indignation, Adam knew Alex had let slip that he was the cause of that black eye.

Since it was early, Adam managed to avoid seeing his mother altogether. Breathing a sigh of relief, he mounted his horse again and rode away, whistling a tune as he turned Caesar toward the Dodwell Academy for Young Ladies.

There was a new groom lounging by the front door, his collar turned up against the strong wind whipping around the corner of the house.

"Glad to see they've hired another groom," said Adam, handing the reins to the young man.

"Haven't," said the youth. "I work for Mr. Edgewood, Mr. David Edgewood, that is."

"Indeed, so is Mr. Edgewood visiting here?"

"That's right, sir, but I'll tend t' your horse for you," he said, spitting on the ground before swinging into the saddle and sending Caesar toward the stables at a spanking pace.

Adam knocked on the door, waiting a full minute before it finally opened slowly. Looking down at him was a giant with blond hair and bright green eyes.

"Yes?" it said.

"Good morning," said Adam, taking a step forward only to stop when the giant didn't step to one side. "I'm Adam Havenhurst. I don't believe we have met."

"Havenhurst? A relative of the Earl of Foxworth?"

So, the giant was familiar with his family tree. Adam smiled and nodded. "My brother, I'm afraid. I'm the vicar here in Pixley."

"Vicar, eh? Step inside."

"Thank you," said Adam, crossing the threshold gingerly. It was difficult getting past the big man, and he was taken aback to discover another giant leaning against the wall just inside.

He held out his hand, saying, "Adam Havenhurst, sir. And you are?"

"I'm James Edgewood. This is my little brother David," the second giant responded, nodding toward the first, who was standing a bit too close for Adam to feel comfortable.

"A pleasure to meet you both. I was wondering if Grace, Miss Edgewood, that is, has come down yet."

"Wait here," said the giant called James.

"This is quite a remarkable school your sister and uncle have here," said Adam with a nervous smile.

"Yes, Uncle Rhodes has told us how much you like the place," said David Edgewood, his green eyes flashing fire for a second.

Adam shifted from one foot to the other and glanced around the grand hall, wishing he had sent a note and arranged a meeting instead.

James Edgewood returned, grinning from ear to ear. Passing Adam, he opened the front door.

"I'm afraid she is unavailable," he said. Though his words were quite impersonal and proper, delivered as if he were a well-trained butler, his jocular expression spoke volumes.

Adam looked down the hallway toward the room James Edgewood had just left. Grace was there, not a hundred feet away, but she was refusing to see him. He found the notion hard to credit.

"If I could just speak to her for a moment . . ."

"I'm afraid not, Vicar. Seems she doesn't want anything to do with anybody named Havenhurst—especially the, uh, priggish one. I assume that means you, since your brother's reputation as a rake and a rogue rather precludes such a description. Sorry, old chap." He swept his large hand toward the front door with a cheerful smile.

"Very well. Tell her . . . oh, never mind. Good day," said Adam, placing his hat on his head and tromping down the front steps. The wind whipped his hat off his head, and he had to lope across the yard after it. He could hear their laughter from behind the closed door. His hat in his hand, he looked around for his curricle and remembered he was on horseback. He turned toward the stable to find Caesar. A chill rain began to fall, and Adam closed his thin coat against the damp. His mood as foul as the day had turned, he stalked around the sprawling house to the stables.

"Good morning, Vicar. What can I do for you?" asked Patrick, looking up from the bridle he was polishing.

Adam dragged his attention away from the empty stable yard and asked, "Where is he? Surely you've not put Caesar in a stall."

"Caesar? Oh, your horse. No, sir, I haven't done anything with him. I haven't even seen him." The groom was clearly puzzled as he watched Adam warily.

"Haven't seen him? Why, I turned him over to that other groom not more than ten minutes ago. Where the devil are they?"

"Not that slackard Pottsby, sir!" said Patrick, setting aside the bridle. Taking no heed of the cold drizzle, the groom strode to the edge of the yard, staring down the empty drive. "The young scoundrel has probably taken him out for a bit of exercise, sir. I'm very sorry. I feel it's my fault. I wouldn't let him stay back here, sitting on his thumbs, doing nothing. So I sent him away. I never thought . . . I'm so sorry, Mr. Havenhurst. I'll saddle up and go and find the rascal."

Adam shook his head, which had started to throb again. "Do not trouble yourself, Patrick. Just saddle me a horse. When the lobcock returns, would you be so good as to bring Caesar back to the vicarage?"

"Very good, sir," said the groom.

"He does know how to ride, I hope," said Adam, watching Patrick throw a saddle on a fine bay mare.

"Oh yes, sir. He's quite competent with the horses, just a fool. I don't know why Mr. Edgewood puts up with him, except that he really is excellent with horses. He's just shiftless."

By this time, Adam was mounted, and his spirits were appeased slightly. "Thank you, Patrick. I'll expect you this afternoon at the latest."

"Thank you, sir," called the groom as Adam rode out of sight.

"Are you certain it was the right thing to do, my dear?" asked Margaret Stiles from her vantage point by the window as she watched the vicar ride off.

Grace had already turned away, her long fingers trailing down the dining room table as she glided gloomily toward the door.

"I cannot bear to see either the earl or the vicar today, Margaret. The one, because he is too insulting and the other, because he is too unspeakably heartless. I'm going to go to class now."

"Yes, do that, my dear. That should occupy your thoughts for a time," said Mrs. Stiles, adding softly, "though it won't cure your broken heart."

Monday afternoon brought a note from the earl, asking Grace's forgiveness for neglecting her and explaining that he was ill.

The next day, another note arrived, accompanied by flowers, but she refused to accept either, sending the earl's footman away with both still in hand. The vicar called, too, but again, she had informed everyone in the household that under no circumstances would she be at home for him.

Grace did not spend her time pining, however. Instead, she kept very busy. She continued with her usual duties, enjoying the added bonus of having two of her brothers there for a visit. Mrs. Brough sent the promised breeches for the girls, and on Wednesday, they began fencing lessons at Dodwell Academy. With James and David present to help, Grace was able to refresh her memory about the sport. It was they who had taught her to fence in the first place, but she had had no opportunity to further her techniques.

The rain stopped, and the stable yard was swept clean of all debris. The foils, with rubber tips, were waiting on a makeshift table. Grace, dressed in knit pantaloons that had once belonged to her brothers, threw open the doors from the drawing room. The breeches-clad girls, giggling and chattering at the promise of a new adventure, gamboled across the stone terrace, through the garden, and into the yard.

When they spied the two Edgewood brothers, they

skidded to a halt, formed a single line, and bowed gravely from the waist.

"Good morning, ladies," said David and James, answering with their own elegant bows. The girls giggled.

Grace watched with fondness as David chose for his first apprentice, the smallest girl, an angelic cherub of ten with dark brown hair and eyes, named Polly.

Squatting down until he was face-to-face with her, David showed her how to hold the foil, his voice low and patient. The other girls listened attentively as he explained the first move, and then stood up, handing the other foil to Grace.

"First, you must salute your opponent. Watch Miss Edgewood. Now, all of you, pretend you have your foil in your hand and do the same. Very good."

"Now, ladies, according to the late George Silver, there are four principles or grounds in fencing—judgment, distance, time, and place. Each is as important as the next, as you will learn when you have been at this awhile. Now, if you can, you want to entice your opponent to come to you. Then you have the choice how to answer his attack. The first is to strike as soon as he, or I suppose I should say she, comes within your place, or range."

"Polly, step toward Miss Edgewood and thrust, so . . ." he said, demonstrating the movement. "Very good. Now, watch what Miss Edgewood does. Parry and forward, thrusting just so! Excellent!"

"Now, ladies, I apologize that I didn't bring enough real foils, but the wooden ones are of a size, so you can learn the science. Later on, Miss Edgewood will be working with only small groups, and the ten I brought should be sufficient. So, choose your weapon and your opponent."

"Grace, you work with the older girls. James and I can handle the younger ones."

"An excellent idea," said Grace, grinning at her brother. She had seen the admiring glances the older girls were giving both her brothers; the last thing either man wanted was to become the object of youthful fantasies. "The following girls will work with me: Diana, Abigail, Amanda, Pamela, Christine, and . . . Olivia, come here at once!" The redheaded girl rolled her eyes and reluctantly joined her friends.

After an hour, Grace called a halt to the lesson. She laughed when her brothers approached her, panting and perspiring.

"It's all that high living you do, you know. Why, you two big, strapping men can't even keep up with a bunch of little girls," she taunted.

James gave one of her blond curls a yank, and David started toward her, rubbing his hands together the way he had done when they were children when he was going to tickle her into submission.

Grace beat a hasty retreat to the house, rushing through the kitchen with unaccustomed haste and up the back flight of stairs. In order to get to her room, she had to cross the lower landing of the wide staircase in the front hall. Panting from her exertions, her shirt damp with perspiration, she was dismayed to hear her name called.

"Grace! Miss Edgewood!"

She froze, turning grudgingly to face the speaker. Here she was, wearing tight knit breeches and a thin white blouse, caught sneaking across the front staircase. Of all the luck! she thought, looking at the vicar with defiance painted on her pursed lips.

"Good morning, Mr. Havenhurst. I'm sorry I cannot visit with you. I have just finished the girls' first fencing lesson, and I must go and change."

"Grace, wait!" he said, bounding up the steps to her side.

He wore a bottle green riding coat and buff-colored breeches, and his cravat was tied in a fashionable knot. His boots shone like new, and Grace wondered idly if he had hired a valet. She shook herself and forced herself to consider some excuse for escape.

Then he took her hand, lifting it to his lips for a brief kiss. "My dear Miss Edgewood, I know you have been avoiding me, and I must say, I don't blame you. But please, you must . . ."

Some of the girls entered the hall from the drawing room, and the vicar immediately released Grace's hand. The girls greeted him respectfully as they filed past, making their way up the stairs to their third-floor rooms. As soon as they were out of sight, their silence dissolved into high-pitched giggles, and the vicar turned a dull red.

Just then, Olivia swept up the stairs and passed by, tossing her red curls and swaying her hips with pointed exaggeration until Grace was moved to say, "Olivia, go to your room at once and stay there until I have come up to speak to you."

"Yes, Miss Edgewood," she said, stomping the remainder of the way up the stairs.

"Now, Mr. Havenhurst, what . . ." she began with icy haughtiness.

Pamela and Diana, shepherding some of the younger girls up the stairs, took their cue from their teacher's manner. Stopping, they clustered around Grace like lionesses protecting their young.

Adam looked from one polite mask to another. Oh, they had learned their lessons well. Even the youngest knew just the correct angle to hold her head to illustrate her disdain for him. Then Grace smiled, and the tableau dissolved.

"Run along, girls, Mr. Havenhurst was just leaving."

The girls continued up the next flight of stairs, leaving Adam alone with Grace.

"Were you looking for us, Mr. Havenhurst?" asked James from the hall below.

Grace's smile widened as Adam grimaced, turning to face her brothers.

"Not exactly," he said. "I came to see your sister; I wanted a word with her."

"Really? With our sister?" said James obtusely.

"Yes," Adam replied.

"Very well, I'm sure you can have a word with her, but perhaps you might call again tomorrow? She seems to have disappeared at the moment."

Adam whirled around to discover that Grace had slipped away. Shaking his head and muttering under his breath, he hurried down the steps and out the front door. At least this time he had had enough sense to merely set the brake on the curricle and slip a feed bag over Caesar's nose. The gelding was none too pleased to have it removed prematurely, but Adam was in no mood for argument.

The occupants of Dodwell Academy were promised to Lord and Lady Briscoe for dinner that evening, a spur-of-the-moment gathering organized when this good lady had learned two more eligible bachelors were visiting in their village. Grace had tried to pretend that she was ill, but her brothers had teased her with the accusation of cowardice until she had finally agreed to attend.

She felt certain Adam would be there, and perhaps the earl, too. To show her utter disregard for either gentleman, Grace chose one of her older gowns, a violet Florence satin. That it showed off her figure to advantage, she couldn't care less, she told herself in the mirror.

The older girls who had been included in the Lamberts' guest list were not invited to this gathering. Olivia looked pointedly at the Edgewood brothers and remarked snidely that it was because Lady Briscoe's spinster sister would be there, trolling for a husband. Grace sent her back to her room for the remainder of the evening. She only wished she could do the same to herself, she thought as she accepted David's hand and climbed into the old coach.

With her brothers there to serve as her escorts, her uncle had declined the invitation. Mrs. Stiles, upon hearing this, developed a sudden headache and announced her intention of remaining behind, leaving Grace to make her excuses with Lady Briscoe.

Grace really didn't mind. Margaret was such a dear, and she couldn't help it if she was head over heels in love with her Uncle Rhodes. Grace wished she could do something to foster a bit more action between the two, but Margaret wouldn't hear of it.

"If Mr. Dodwell doesn't realize how I feel, then no one is going to tell him," Mrs. Stiles had said time and again.

Grace wondered idly if she would be saying the same thing in twenty years—about herself and the vicar—not that she admitted . . . At any rate, the thought did nothing to lift her spirits.

The drive to the Briscoes' estate took half an hour, and the occupants of the coach were thoroughly chilled by the time they arrived. When they entered the drawing room, Grace breathed a sigh of relief. Neither one of her nemeses were present, and she brightened, prepared to enjoy the outing.

She found herself singled out by Lady Briscoe's sister, the spinster Olivia had so recently insulted. Annabelle Pruitt had been at school with Grace, though Grace had been in the younger class. But she greeted Grace like a long-lost, bosom friend, linking arms with her and chatting as they paraded the perimeter of the room. Grace had difficulty containing her amusement as she recalled Olivia's very apt description of Annabelle's activity.

At the far end of the drawing room, they stopped and Annabelle's conversation became even louder and more animated. Grace glanced at her brother, who was standing by the open terrace door, blowing a cloud with their host. She tilted her head to signal him, and he grinned, but he took her hint, handing his cigar to Lord Briscoe and approaching them with exaggerated eagerness.

"And you must be the divine Miss Pruitt my sister mentioned to me earlier," said James, bowing over her hand.

"Annabelle, may I present my brother James," said Grace, waiting a few minutes before turning to make her escape.

She walked straight into the broad chest of Adam Havenhurst.

"You," she whispered. "I do not want to hear a single word on a single subject from you, Mr. Havenhurst."

"Good evening, Miss Edgewood," he said politely, stepping back and saying to his mother, "You remember Miss Edgewood, do you not, Mother?"

"Miss Edgewood? Of course I do. Are you certain you are feeling quite the thing?" demanded the matron, startling Grace, who thought the countess was addressing her. She grinned when she realized Adam was the target of that comment.

Placing her gloved hand on his forehead, Lady Foxworth demanded imperiously, "You aren't coming down with a fever, too, are you? I told you this air in the country would not be beneficial to you, my boy. Really, I think I should write to the bishop and demand that he find you a replacement."

"Mother, I am not ill, I do not have a fever, and I do not want to leave Pixley!" he snapped, his voice rising and causing heads to turn.

"Adam, I . . . oh, my vinaigrette," wailed the countess, causing her son to turn scarlet—whether from embarrassment or anger, Grace was not certain. She took the opportunity to slip away again, a fact that proved to be a restorative to the countess, who took her son's arm and led him to the opposite end of the well-appointed room.

Dinner was announced, and they adjourned to the dining room to find their places. Grace breathed a sigh of relief when she realized that she and Adam were seated on the same side of the table, but at opposite ends. She wouldn't even have to look at him, she thought smugly, and then wondered the rest of the meal if he was enjoying having Annabelle Pruitt as his dinner companion.

For Grace, Lady Briscoe had selected the squire and Richard Lambert. The former was too engrossed in the excellent assortment of dishes to do more than smack his lips and recommend the occasional entrée to her. The latter, deprived of Pamela and the other young ladies, decided that she was not quite as ancient as he had imagined, and tried to charm her. His efforts were merely an irritating distraction from her troubled reflections.

Grace had spent three days denying Adam entrance to her home, hoping to purge him from her thoughts. She now knew such an event was highly unlikely. It seemed the Honorable Adam Havenhurst had taken up residence in her heart and was not likely to be shaken loose. One look into those dark brown eyes had been all it took to enslave her again. She was his for the asking. She thrust her chin out defiantly, effectively silencing the verbose young man by her side, and vowed to herself that she would not bow down before him, nor would she retreat from her convictions.

She wouldn't play the lightskirt for his brother, and she certainly wouldn't change into some milk-and-water miss without a thought in her head for him. He could have her, but he would have to take her as she was!

Having made this resolution, Grace turned a blinding smile on Richard Lambert, which made him drop his wineglass, splashing the red liquid all over his tulip pink waistcoat.

The ladies left the gentlemen to their port and returned to the drawing room. Adam pulled a small notebook out of his pocket and began composing a note to Grace. If she refused to speak to him, perhaps he could intrigue her with a note.

"What's that you've got there, Vicar," said Lord Briscoe, who was, for once, sober as a judge.

"What?" he asked, thinking feverishly. "Oh, I just thought of something I wanted to include in Sunday's sermon. Thought I'd jot it down so I wouldn't forget."

"Good idea," said his host, moving back down the table and stopping to speak to the squire.

"Quite a large thought," said James, glancing toward the paper. Adam smiled slightly and turned to keep his words hidden.

"I guess you have to write it down when the spirit moves you," added the giant.

"Just so," he murmured, wishing Grace's brother would leave him alone. But his luck was quite out. Instead, the other brother drifted over and stood, looming over the table and Adam's small notebook. With a loud sigh, he closed it and put it back in his pocket.

"We are acquainted with your brother," said David, sitting down and taking a long pull on his cigar, expelling the smoke so that it drifted upward in little rings.

"Five rings," he said, cocking his head toward his brother James in challenge.

Soon, the three men were enveloped in smoke as the two brothers tried to outdo each other. Adam stood up,

about to make good his escape, when strong fingers
closed around his wrist.

"A word in your ear, Vicar," said James, releasing him
when he glared down at the hand. "As far as I'm concerned, your brother's reputation with the ladies prevents
him from being suitable company for our sister. You'll
tell him for us, won't you?"

Adam smiled down at the twin giants and nodded,
saying, "I assure you, gentlemen, I couldn't agree more,
and so I have already told him."

James and David exchanged puzzled glances. James
spoke for them and said, "We thought that was why you
were trying to see Grace, for your brother."

Adam stiffened, but he didn't speak.

David rose and clapped him on the back. "Just a misunderstanding, Mr. Havenhurst. Know you'll forgive us.
After all, that's your job, isn't it?" Chuckling at his witticism, David pulled James away to join the other gentlemen, who were drifting slowly toward the drawing room.

Adam sat down and completed the note in private. He
read over it, displeased by the coldness, but perhaps that
was what Grace needed from him. At least he had re-
frained from any mention of fencing, bathing, or
breeches. He added another line, asking her to meet
him . . .

Adam chewed on the end of his pencil a moment.
Where could they possibly meet that they wouldn't be
spotted by one of their gossipy neighbors or giggling
students?

Of course! he thought. Mrs. Odstock had said she
needed leave on Thursday to take care of her sick mother.
He had granted it, of course, but he had wondered how
a woman of Mrs. Odstock's advanced years could possibly have a mother still alive. Now, he said a quick
prayer for the ancient mother; Grace could come to the
vicarage in the morning.

Suddenly he frowned. How could he convince her to come to his house when he couldn't even manage to have a conversation with her? She would simply not show up.

There had to be another place. Suddenly, Adam smiled. The bathhouse. It was the perfect place for their assignation. It was on her territory so she shouldn't feel threatened. And at night, it would be completely private. The thought of being able to see Grace alone, that very night, made him smile.

Whistling, he finished the note and folded it before joining the other guests in the drawing room.

His mother was dozing on the sofa, sprawled across one end in an unladylike pose, although no one would dare wake her to tell her so. The gathering was much more pleasant without her constant harping anyway.

Grace was playing the pianoforte, with Richard Lambert gazing wide-eyed at her while he turned the pages. Adam noticed in amusement that she was getting quite vexed with having to prod him each time; her playing was mediocre enough without the added distraction of stopping at the end of each page.

Adam turned to the squire and engaged him in desultory conversation, all the while keeping an eye on his quarry. Occasionally, he fancied that Grace was casting him longing glances, but he didn't wish to put it to the test. He felt unequal to the humiliation of another public rejection.

Lady Briscoe called for card tables to be set up, and Adam found himself partnering his hostess. His mother, he noticed in dismay, had perked up at the sound of cards being shuffled and had latched on to the squire as a partner for whist. The stakes were pitiably low, and he hoped that would keep his mother from getting up to her old tricks. He had discounted, however, his mother's keen passion for competition. She invited James Edgewood and the silly Millicent Lambert to join them.

As for Grace, she was seated at the next table, where he might gaze at her, in profile, as much as he wished. Lady Briscoe chided him for his inattention to worldly matters, but he only smiled.

After half an hour, Adam heard James Edgewood mutter something under his breath. Glancing at his mother, who was dealing the cards, Adam grimaced and shook his head. His dark, troubled eyes met James's; the communication was immediate. James smiled and nodded, returning his attention to the table. If the squire guessed that his partner, the Countess of Foxworth, was cheating at whist, he wasn't going to protest; his daughter, Millicent, was too much of a ninnyhammer to notice. And James Edgewood, whom he would gladly have consigned to the devil earlier in the evening, knew, but had no intention of dragging the Foxworth family skeleton out of its closet.

Still, it wouldn't do to let his mother fleece her benefactor, and after an hour, Adam rose and called it quits. His mother pouted, but the country party had gone on later than most, by Pixley's standards. Soon, the rest of the guests began gathering up their belongings, making a general exodus toward the front door.

Adam placed his mother's cloak around her shoulders and turned to find Grace. She was already out the front door, and he had to elbow his way through the crowd to reach her in time. As her brother James was closing the carriage door, Adam grabbed his hand, shaking it firmly and transferring the note from his palm to Grace's brother's.

James frowned at the folded note in his hand, then understanding dawned, and he nodded.

"Vicar, you'll be sure to tell your mother I enjoyed our little game," he said with a wink for Adam.

"Oh yes, I'll tell her," said Adam. "And you'll take care of that other matter?"

"You can count on me," said James, closing the door and calling, "Let's go home, Patrick!"

It was almost midnight when the carriage pulled up to the front door. The lights in the study were still burning; puzzled that her uncle would still be awake, Grace opened the door, starting at the sight of Mrs. Stiles sitting on the edge of her uncle's chair.

Smiling brightly, she shook her finger at the couple and demanded with mock severity, "What is the meaning of all this?"

"Well, well, well, Uncle," said James, following Grace into the room.

David, peering over his brother's shoulder, added, "Oh, I say!"

Margaret would have risen, but Uncle Rhodes had his arm about her waist and was not letting go. Blushing, she remained where she was.

"You may wish us happy, children," Uncle Rhodes said, grinning from ear to ear. "Mrs. Stiles has kindly agreed to accept my hand in marriage."

"Mr. Dodwell!" she exclaimed giving his chest a playful push. He captured her hand and brought it to his lips.

Grace rushed forward, embracing them both. "How wonderful! Absolutely wonderful!" she exclaimed before her breath caught in her throat.

"What is it, my dear?" asked her uncle.

"Nothing, nothing. I am just so happy for you both. So happy," she finished in a whisper. Pasting a bright smile on her face, she said, "Well, when is it going to be?"

"Very soon, I hope. I'm not getting any younger, you know," said her uncle.

"Congratulations," chorused the brothers, kissing their

new aunt on her pink cheek and shaking their uncle's hand.

"Champagne!" said James.

"Oh dear, I'm afraid all the servants are abed," said Margaret.

"Never fear, we shall go foraging! Come along, David."

"I am right behind you!"

The two disappeared, leaving Grace alone with the beaming couple.

"I am delighted for you both," she said, a wobbly smile on her face.

"Thank you, my dear," said her uncle. Rising, he put his arm around her, standing on tiptoe to kiss her cheek. "That means a great deal to both of us."

"Thank you. I—I must go—I," she stuttered, and hurried out the door.

"I'll go to her," said Margaret.

"No, give her time, my dear. She's not upset about us, and you can't help with the other. It's best to leave her to herself," he said, giving her waist an intimate squeeze.

Grace climbed the stairs, calling a weary good night to her brothers, who were heading back to their uncle's study, a bottle of champagne held before them like a trophy.

"What? Not staying for the toast?" asked James.

"I'll toast them tomorrow," she said, continuing on her way.

Grace went straight to her room, changed into her nightgown, and climbed into bed. A delightful end to a very long day. Recalling the look of love on the faces of the two people she held most dear—except for one other, perhaps—she smiled and hugged her pillow to her chest. She fought the illogical tears and forced herself to clear her mind, giving in to the fatigue. Within minutes, she was sound asleep.

* * *

When they reached the road, Adam told his mother's coachman to "spring 'em," and the well-sprung carriage flew toward the vicarage.

"Adam, really, tell him to slow down or I shall have a fit of the vapors."

"As well you should, madam. You should be ashamed of yourself, fleecing our neighbors like you were," said Adam severely.

"I have no idea what you are talking about," she began haughtily. Then, her tone petulant, she added, "And I don't know how you can speak to your mother like that. You sound more and more like Foxworth. I shan't always be around for the two of you to abuse."

Adam, whose heart was racing at the prospect of meeting Grace, was too excited to react to his mother's theatrics. Breathing a sigh of relief as they pulled up to the vicarage, he jumped out of the carriage.

"Good night, Mother," he called, giving the coachman the signal to proceed.

"Adam, aren't you . . ." her words were carried away as the carriage lumbered off.

Whistling, Adam hurried through the cottage and out to the stable, where Caesar greeted him with a sleepy whiny of protest. Adam harnessed him to the curricle and drove out of the yard and into the road. Glancing up at the three-quarter moon, Adam blew it a kiss.

There would be no mistakes this time, he thought as he passed the gates of Dodwell Academy and bowled up the drive, passing the house and continuing on until he arrived at the bathhouse. The sight of the stone structure sent a chill of foreboding down his spine, but Adam shook off the feeling. Climbing down, he could hear someone splashing water. He frowned, wondering why on earth Grace would have chosen to swim on such a raw night. He tried the door, but it was locked.

Had he made a mistake? Perhaps she was refusing to meet with him. But it had to be her inside. Who else would have business in the bathhouse at one o'clock in the morning. He raised his hand to knock, but something held him back. What if it wasn't Grace inside?

Adam paced back and forth between the bathhouse and the curricle, considering his options. He could simply go home, but that was the coward's way out. Faint heart ne'er won fair maid, or some such foolishness. But what other choice did he have?

He had simply assumed Grace would meet him, and would leave the door unlocked. Reaching into his pocket, he pulled out a small knife and unfolded it. It was the sort a gentleman used to clean his fingernails or cut off a slice of apple. It had also come in handy when he had been at school, would go out for a lark, and find himself locked out for the night. He stuck the blade into the keyhole, working it this way and that until he heard a distinctive click.

Inside, only one fire had been lit, and the lamps on the walls were dark. The air was thick from condensation, and his eyes had trouble adjusting.

He peered into the pool; he thought he could just make out a figure, under the water, swimming rapidly toward him. Adam leaned closer. Suddenly, he realized there were three figures, and he frowned in confusion, not moving away until it was too late. The three figures surfaced as one, gasping for air and laughing, too.

"Grace?"

Screams in three different pitches pierced the silence of the night. As one, the figures in the pool moved, and a wall of water rose out of the pool, catching him by surprise and soaking him thoroughly. The screaming continued although the figures were sloshing away from him now. Adam took to his heels and ran, slipping on the slick surface and skidding toward the closed door. He threw it open and made good his escape. Leaping into his curricle and releasing the brake, Caesar must have caught his master's urgency for he leapt forward like the demons of hell were on his heels.

Adam could hear the uproar of screaming girls and the deeper-voiced shouts of Grace's brothers. He only hoped they weren't armed, and didn't try to follow. He had had enough for one night!

The trip back to the vicarage was accomplished in record time. After giving Caesar a good rubdown, Adam entered the house and stripped off his coat, falling across the bed, completely exhausted.

A violent sneeze forced him to rise and remove his wet clothes. Another sneeze exploded, this one followed by a mild curse. He was shivering by the time he managed to light the fire in the fireplace. He climbed back into bed and pulled up the covers, wishing he had accepted his mother's offer of more blankets.

"I think they will be all right now," whispered Margaret, closing the door on the room where Olivia, Diana, and Pamela slept. "That was quite an ordeal. I know they should not have gone down there without permission, and so late, too, but what a terrible experience for them."

"Yes, I shall have Mr. Gray come out tomorrow and reinforce the locks on the doors," said Grace, holding the candle high to light their way to their own rooms.

"Perhaps a bolt on the inside would be wise," said the older woman, smoothing her gray hair and yawning. "Well, good night, my dear."

"Good night, Margaret. I think we will forego morning classes."

"An excellent notion."

Grace had been shaken out of a sound sleep and now all she wanted was to return to her bed. The girls' screams, followed by wrenching sobs, had been traumatic for everyone. Uncle Rhodes, dressed in his nightshirt and cap, had declared that he wouldn't rest until he saw the culprit hung on Tyburn Hill.

David had immediately begun searching the grounds, but James had remained strangely silent. Grace frowned when she recalled this curious detail. James was usually in the middle of any call for action.

Just then, there was a quiet knock on her door, and Grace suffered a moment's hesitation before padding silently across the room to open it. It annoyed her that the events of the evening had unnerved her so.

"James? What is it? Have you found something?"

"No, no," he said, entering the room without looking at her. "Nice room."

"You didn't come in here to tell me that."

"No, it's about tonight."

"Really, James, I don't think I can bear anything else about tonight. I told the girls it was probably Richard Lambert and his cronies, but I don't believe it for a moment." She had thought of Adam, but that was ridiculous.

"Well, I think I know what happened," he said, hanging his head and shuffling his feet. He held out his hand and opened it. "I was supposed to give this to you, but you went straight up to bed and I forgot. I haven't read it, but I'm afraid I should have. If I had, perhaps this evening's conclusion would have been very different."

Grace took the note and opened it, digesting it quickly. She sagged against the wall for support.

"I was right. I should have read it. Can you forgive me?" he asked, the penitence in his voice pleading with her in a way words could not. When she neither spoke nor looked up at him, he asked again, "Grace, can you forgive me?"

Her shoulders started to shake, and she looked up, her eyes bright with laughter.

"Forgive you, brother? Why I'm going to kiss you!" And she stood on tiptoes and gave his cheek a resounding kiss. " 'Good night, sweet prince,' " she quoted gaily as she pushed him out the door.

Grace flew across the room and bounded onto the bed, hugging her knees to her chest. Then she opened her hand and smoothed out the note, holding it close to the candle on the table by the bed, and reading every precious word again.

> *My dear Miss Edgewood,*
> *I know in the past, you have often had reason to be angry with me, but I hope you can set this prejudice aside and will agree to meet with me. There is something very particular which I must say to you. In* private. *I will meet you in the bathhouse one hour after we leave this gathering.*
> > *Yr Servant,*
> > *Adam Havenhurst*

Pressing the precious note to her lips, Grace placed it under her pillow and laid down her head. She would go to him first thing in the morning. Perhaps she could get there before that awful Mrs. Odstock arrived for the day.

With a gentle smile curving her lips, Grace slept better than she had in weeks.

Ten

"Grace, wake up, wake up!"

The voice simply would not go away, and Grace finally opened her eyes to bright sunshine. She blinked and tried to focus on the face staring down at her.

"Hurry, you must get dressed," said Margaret, taking a gown from the maid's hands and laying it across the bed. "Her ladyship will not like to be kept waiting. I thought the Quality didn't rise until afternoon."

"Her ladyship?" moaned Grace, flopping back against the pillow. Suddenly, she recalled the note and snatched it from its hiding place. She read it again and expelled a happy sigh.

"Yes, the Countess of Foxworth has called and is asking for you, my dear. It's practically a royal summons," said Margaret Stiles.

"The Countess of Foxworth!" exclaimed Grace, spurred to action at the thought of *his* mother paying a call—and so very early in the morning. "What time is it?" she asked, bathing her face and drying it hurriedly.

"It's almost eleven o'clock."

Grace's movements slowed as she digested this tidbit of news, but she continued to allow Margaret to poke and prod her until she was credibly turned out and ready to greet their visitor.

When she entered the small drawing room that they

kept for visitors, Grace could feel the chill emanating from the countess. She was wearing black this morning, including a black veil, and Grace was assailed by the unthinkable prospect that something horrible had happened to Adam on his way home from that disastrous encounter in the bathhouse.

"My lady, what has happened?" she asked, rushing to the sofa.

The countess glared at her. Grace took a deep breath and moved back a pace; this was not the visit of a bereaved mother.

"Happened? I was going to ask you the same thing, Miss Edgewood," she said, her thin nose elevated to an absurd height. "It was bad enough when Foxworth became indisposed and refused to stir from his room. He hasn't been downstairs all week, you know."

"No, I had no idea," said Grace, removing to the chair beside the sofa and perching on the edge of the seat.

"I'm surprised. He told me he was paying you a visit, and when he returned, he went straight to his room and hasn't left it. But that is not the worst of your machinations."

"Machinations?" Grace gasped, unsure if she should be amused or incensed.

"Yes, I have just come from Adam's cottage. He has been ill, a slight cold. I was worried about him after the way he acted last night, rushing me away from the card party and speaking so . . . never you mind about that. I know he didn't stay home after I dropped him off. I had my coachman stop just down the road, and what do you suppose I saw not ten minutes later?"

"I'm sure I don't know," she lied. Obviously, she had witnessed Adam's departure for Dodwell Academy. Grace's brow puckered, and she bit at her lower lip. She hoped the countess had not followed Adam and watched the debacle at the bathhouse, but the dowager's next words dispelled this worry.

"He drove out of his drive and turned his carriage toward this place."

"Lady Foxworth, why would you assume Adam came here? Perhaps he found a note from someone who needed his help. He is the vicar, you know," said Grace, earning a snort of derision.

"I know he is the vicar of this insignificant little hamlet, but that is not what happened. I just came from the vicarage. Adam was sitting in his tiny little kitchen sipping tepid tea, too weak from fever to fix a proper cup."

"He didn't appear that ill last night at Lord and Lady Briscoe's dinner," said Grace.

"He is much too noble to trouble others with his ill health. But this morning, he could not hide it from his mother. He is much worse today, and is it any wonder when he comes rooting around here at all hours, doing who knows what! I found his soaked clothes in his room, and that was enough for me." The countess rose and sailed to the door.

"Both my sons! Stricken down by a . . . schoolmistress," she said, endowing the final word with loathing.

Grace followed but did not attempt further conversation with the countess. She wouldn't have listened anyway. After a polite good-bye, which the countess ignored completely, Grace hurried to the kitchen and asked Cook to put up some of the day's soup for her to take to the ailing vicar. While Cook was packing a basket that contained a week's worth of food and other restoratives, Grace sent one of the maids to the stable to ask Patrick to harness the pony to the trap. Then she went upstairs to fetch her cloak and bonnet.

Grace's journey took her through the village, and she stopped to see the blacksmith about adding an inside bolt to the bathhouse.

"I'd be happy to, Miss Edgewood," said Mr. Gray, "and I won't even charge you for it."

"Of course I will pay you, Mr. Gray," replied Grace.

"No, no, if the key lock I put on there to begin with has broken, I'm going to make things right."

"But it's not broken," she said, her cheeks turning crimson as she continued, stammering, "that is, it just isn't—well, we would like—I mean, someone could—"

He was watching her, his expression wolfish. Grace took a deep breath and said primly, "Just see to the lock, Mr. Gray, and send me the bill."

"Very good, miss," said the blacksmith, grinning from ear to ear.

"Good day to you," she called, touching old Sissy on the neck with her whip and urging her forward. The entire village would be dining on this conversation before noon. Grace forced a smile when she spied Mr. Crane, and she nodded to Miss Silverton, who waved and then hurried off in the direction she had come from. Glancing over her shoulder, Grace saw Mr. Gray, *sans* his leather apron, already hurrying toward his friends to tell them the news of Miss Edgewood's strange, blushing request. Turning the pony trap to take the west road to the vicarage, she rolled her eyes. They would draw their own conclusions about her destination!

Grace had never allowed the village gossip to worry her overmuch, and this morning, its power over her was completely void. Nothing could dampen her spirits. Adam wanted to see her, to tell her something very particular. She sighed and hummed a little tune, her smile widening when she recognized the naughty melody that had shocked the vicar so. Not the vicar, she amended, her vicar, her Adam. She burst into song at this, singing the lyrics her brothers—her dear, sweet brothers—had taught her:

I hae been blythe wi' comrades dear
I hae been merry drinking.
I hae been joyful gath'rin' gear
I hae been happy thinking.
But a' the pleasures e'er I saw
Tho' three times doubled fairly,
That happy night was worth them a'
Amang the rigs wi' . . . Adam.

Glancing left and right to be certain her foolishness had not been observed, Grace giggled like one of her students, and sang lustily, "A . . . dam!"

Her laughter lasted until she came around the bend and found herself face-to-face with Richard Lambert on horseback. He was not riding, merely sitting on his horse . . . listening.

Grace cringed, but she pulled back on the reins and said brightly, "Good morning, Mr. Lambert."

"Good morning, Miss Edgewood. I heard you singing," he said, a sly grin on his youthful face.

"Yes, I'm afraid I get a little carried away on a morning such as this."

"I understand, Miss Edgewood, I understand. On your way to see the vicar?" he asked.

"I may drop in, Mr. Lambert," she said, giving him a frosty stare.

But the man was young and unaccustomed to obeying Society's strictures, and he probed further, saying, "I saw Mrs. Odstock on her way to her mother's earlier. The poor woman is quite ill, you know."

"Yes, I do seem to recall. If you'll excuse me," said Grace, raising her brows in a manner that made her students cringe.

On the young man, it failed to have the desired effect, but he tipped his hat to her and pulled to one side of the road to allow her to pass.

"Good day, Miss Edgewood. Give my regards to the vicar," he called after her.

Grace did not respond, but she wished she had said something very cutting when his laughter followed her down the road.

Ignore it, she told herself. Ignore Richard Lambert and John Gray, and all the villagers. They just enjoyed a good gossip; they were not really malicious, and she knew they wished her well. She was quite fond of them all— except the viperish Miss Silverton—and knew they were fond of her also. Let them have their little gossip. She didn't care, she thought, as she turned into the neat little yard in front of the vicarage.

With a light step, Grace picked up the pot of soup and went to the door. She knocked softly, repeating this more forcefully.

Finally, the door opened, and she stepped back, surprised to find Adam wearing only a dressing gown. No, not only that, she realized as the untied garment flopped open, revealing his inexpressibles. Having grown up with four brothers, Grace didn't even blush, but she was glad when he began tying the dressing gown—that broad, bare chest was taking her breath away.

"Good morning, Vicar," she said, smiling into those dark eyes.

Adam sniffed, opened his mouth to speak, and turned away as a mighty sneeze shook his body.

"What do you want?" came his terse response.

"I have brought you some soup," she said, entering the small parlor. She faced him, studying him fondly from his stubbly chin and disheveled copper curls to his sweet, soulful eyes—except they were gazing at her with an expression that was anything but sweet.

"I received your note," she whispered, suddenly unsure of the wisdom of visiting him.

"Yes, I gathered as much last night. That was quite a

reception you planned for me. Did you tell them I was coming, or did you decide their part should be unrehearsed?"

Frowning, Grace said, "I don't know what you mean." Then she chuckled and added, "Oh, you mean the girls. No, no, they had no idea you were coming."

He took a step back and said, "I am amazed, Miss Edgewood. Amazed and shocked! Even you should grasp the impropriety in allowing your students to be party to such a farce. I thought better of you, but I can see I was mistaken. Anyone who would jeopardize the children under her care . . . well, words cannot express my disappointment. Please leave." Thrusting his nose in the air in a pose reminiscent of his mother, he opened the door wide and waited.

But Grace was not ready to leave. She refused to allow him to think that she could behave so callously, so improperly.

"Adam, let me explain. This is all a big misunderstanding. I did receive your note, but not until after all the commotion was over and done."

Shifting the small iron pot to one hand, she placed the other hand on his silk brocade dressing gown. Adam jerked his arm away. Tears sprang to her eyes, but she tried once again.

"James forgot to give me the note. Please, Adam, do not be like this."

Reaching into the pocket of her gown, she held out the note he had written, saying, "In your note, you say you have something very particular to tell me. Won't you tell me now?"

The eyes looking into hers were hooded, devoid of all emotion. His jaw clenched and unclenched. Then he said coldly, "Very well, Miss Edgewood. Your plan to hold out for higher stakes will not work. I wanted to warn you that my brother has no intention of offering you marriage. It will be a carte blanche or nothing, so you needn't pin your hopes so high."

"Your brother . . . carte blanche . . . he told you!" she sputtered, anger taking over her despair. "Why, you patronizing, foppish, popinjay! How dare you think I would ever . . . your brother can . . . and if you think I'd ever want you to . . . oh!" she shouted, shoving the pot of soup at his chest and rushing toward the door.

Adam tried to catch it, but missed. The heavy iron pot landed squarely on his foot, splashing hot liquid up to his knees. Howling in pain, and hopping on his good foot, Adam slammed the door.

Grace leapt into her trap, picked up the reins, and jerked them around, picking up the whip and popping old Sissy's rump. The old horse whinnied her protest and jumped forward, knocking down the freshly painted fence and trampling the newly planted shrubbery as she carried her mistress away.

When she was out of sight of the house, Grace pulled back on the reins, letting the old horse rest. She listened in vain for the sound of pursuit, but only silence greeted her. Grace was not so upset that she returned home the way she had come. Instead, she took the long way, avoiding the village altogether. The journey took over an hour, but she didn't encounter anyone along the way—a blessing since every time she thought she was over her tears, new worries would open the floodgates again.

So, it was truly over; all her hopes had shriveled and died. She told herself a dozen times that she hoped never to see either Havenhurst brother ever again. And every time she made this vow, the tears began afresh. The earl, of course, could take himself back to London and never show his face in Pixley again, for all she cared. Adam . . .

Grace angrily dashed away the tears again.

She managed to have a brittle smile on her face for Patrick when she reached the stable yard, but it was short-lived. Once inside the house, she ran into her two brothers and again dissolved into tears.

Alarmed, James put his arms around her and demanded, "What's happened, little sister? I thought you'd be walking on clouds by now. John Gray came from the village to measure for a new lock on the bathhouse, and he was quite beside himself with the news of your visit to the vicarage."

"We thought we would be wishing you happy by now," said David.

"Well, you needn't bother!" snapped Grace, sniffing loudly.

"Now, now, come and tell us all about it," said James, placing a bracing arm around her shoulders and leading her toward her uncle's study.

Grace shook herself free and backed away, saying bravely, "Your wanting to help is very kind, James, but there is nothing you can do. I would appreciate it if you wouldn't mention any of this again."

"If you're sure, then mum's the word."

"Thank you," she whispered, turning away and rushing up the stairs to the privacy of her room.

The two brothers looked at each other and nodded. Grabbing their hats and coats, they headed out the door.

"My dear boy, whatever has happened here?" demanded the dowager countess, stepping back in horror at the sight of her precious son on his hands and knees, scrubbing the parlor floor.

Adam looked up at her sideways and said with awful sarcasm, "I do believe I am cleaning up a pot of soup, Mother. Vegetable soup, to be more precise." Using his hands, he picked up the squashed remains of a carrot and pitched it back into the soup pot. "Would you care to help?"

"Adam! Do not be ridiculous, and pray, get off your knees. Where is that woman of yours, that Mrs. Oddjob?" she said, plucking at his shoulder.

"Mrs. Odstock, Mother, and she has gone to visit her sick mother for the day."

"Well, that is very inconsiderate of her to go off and leave you with a mess to clean. Do, please, get up, Adam. I cannot bear to see you doing that. And here you are sick. You haven't even the strength to dress yourself properly. I daresay you will end up on your deathbed."

Adam grinned and rose, a little devil inside prodding him to say, "I should think so, Mother, just like everyone else."

She put her hand to his forehead, and whined, "Oh, do not tease your poor mother so. Have you no regard for my delicate sensibilities? With you gone, what will become of me?"

"I'm sorry, Mother," he said obediently, but he pushed her hand away and helped her cross the threshold, which was still slippery with soup. "What did you want, Mother? After you paid me a visit this morning—an inordinately early visit, I might add—I expected you to take to your bed with a case of the vapors."

"As if I could allow myself such a luxury when you are suffering from a raging fever." She sighed, sitting down in the one soft chair and carefully arranging her black skirts. "No, I decided to come and wait here for the physician to arrive."

"The physician? I don't need a physician. I have a bit of a cold, that's all."

Ignoring his comment, as she usually did, the countess continued. "I happen to know that Dr. Smyth-Edwards is visiting an estate in the next county. I have sent for him to attend to you, and to your brother, too."

"Mother, I do wish you would not have done so," said Adam, frowning when he considered the last part of her speech. "But why does Alex need to see a doctor? He is not ill."

"He most certainly is. I told you he has refused to come out of his room all week. He says he is afraid of giving me whatever ails him. Most obliging, of course, but I think it has been long enough. He, too, will see Dr. Smyth-Edwards."

"Mother, Alex is not ill. He is merely nursing a sore stomach and a black eye." At her gasp, he chuckled and added, "A black eye which I gave him the last time he came here."

"Oh, Adam, he did not hurt you, did he?" she demanded anxiously.

"Really, Mother, have you no sympathy for your first-born?"

"If he provoked you to violence, I'm certain he deserved it," said the countess, further astounding her son. "But why is his stomach sore?"

Shaking his head, Adam grinned and said without thinking, "Grace gave him one in the breadbasket."

"Miss Edgewood again! I might have known! Well, I will take care of her, never fear."

Adam grabbed his mother by the shoulders and demanded, "What do you mean, you'll take care of her?"

"I mean that sometimes a mother must stand up for her children, and so I told her this morning. Please, Adam, you will give me bruises."

Releasing her, he asked, "Where did you see Miss Edgewood, Mother?"

"After I left you here, I went to visit her. I knew you went to her house last night, after I dropped you here. I had the coachman wait to see why you were in such a hurry to get home. I shan't question you too closely about it, for I am too much of a lady, unlike someone I won't mention, to even speculate on what you might have been doing there—and with her."

Adam leaned against the wall, his strength completely sapped. He had always known his mother was high-handed, but he had never guessed the extent of her manipulations.

Looking down at her, he was moved to action. "Mother, let me help you up."

"I am not leaving until you have seen the doctor."

"Yes, Mother, you are, because I am not going to see the doctor. I am going to see Miss Edgewood and apologize to her for whatever you might have said to her this morning. Hopefully, you were not too outrageously rude since she was thoughtful enough to bring me a pot of soup."

"I might have known that hussy had something to do with your being forced to scrub the floor!"

"Enough, Mother. I will not hear another word against Miss Edgewood. She may not forgive us for our discourtesy, but I am going to beg, if I must, on bended knee."

"You mustn't, Adam! Knowing her, she will think it is a declaration! I forbid you to go anywhere near her, Adam," she said, clinging to his arm. "She's not at all the type of woman you, a vicar, should associate with. Why, Mrs. Brough told me that she made up three dozen pairs of breeches for the girls at that school. Can you imagine what those poor girls are learning from that . . . that . . . ?"

"She is teaching them grace and poise, Mother, through the science of fencing. That is all, and I'm certain there's nothing wrong with a group of girls being dressed in breeches for such an activity. It is not as if they are going to a ball wearing men's inexpressibles."

"Adam! Language!"

"Yes, Mother, language, something I should have used years ago to tell you that I will not tolerate your meddling in my affairs any longer. You are welcome to remain at Foxworth Manor, in Pixley, but I will not allow you to either control or manipulate me or my affairs any longer. And if I should be lucky enough to have Grace listen to me, I fully intend to make a declaration. I love her, and I hope she may feel the same about me."

"Love, oh, Adam! Where did you come by such bourgeois notions," she cried.

"You are nothing, if not predictable," said Adam, shaking his head. Then, his movements purposeful, he said, "Now, let me help you past this mess so that I can finish cleaning it up. Good day, Mother."

She placed the back of her hand against her forehead as if she was about to faint, and he put an arm around her waist, half carrying her out to the carriage.

When he had seen her safely deposited on the velvet squabs, he patted her hand and said more patiently, "You have been my champion for many years, Mother, but I am a man now and wish to do things for myself—alone. I will come to call in a few days."

She turned her head and gazed forlornly out the opposite window. Adam closed the door and stood back from the carriage.

"Take her back to Foxworth Manor, Harry." The coachman lifted his whip in salute and sent the horses on their way.

Adam went inside and finished cleaning the soup off the parlor floor. Then he went upstairs to dress. The shirt was no problem, but his leg was red and tender where the soup had burned it, and he groaned as he tried to pull on the knit breeches. Finally, he gave up and rummaged through one of the trunks his mother had insisted he needed until he found a pair of black Cossack trousers which were loose-fitting and reached the ankle. They were fashionable in London, of course, but he hadn't considered them appropriate for country wear.

Standing back and inspecting himself in the warped mirror, Adam shook his head. It was hardly his usual mode of attire, but it would have to do, he thought. Next, footwear.

Looking down at his bare feet, he grimaced. The one the soup pot had landed on was swollen and discolored, and he knew he would never be able to get his boots on. Pulling out his black shoes, he pushed and prodded until the swollen foot was securely enclosed.

Having no claim to being fashionable like his brother, Adam made short work of his cravat. After shrugging into his coat and brushing his hair, he declared himself ready.

"Anybody home?"

Adam limped to the stairs and called, "I'll be down in a moment. Make yourself comfortable."

The stairs were hard to navigate with his aching foot, and the baggy trousers kept flopping against the tender skin on his shin. Adam grimaced as he realized that getting around was going to be a great trial for a few days. By the time he reached the parlor, a fine film of perspiration covered his brow. Finding the small room filled by Grace's treelike brothers did nothing to bolster his self-confidence.

He started by holding up his hand and declaring stoutly, "I am in no mood to hear . . ."

"What did you do to Grace?" demanded David, stepping closer and peering down his nose at Adam.

Adam, not one to be intimidated, glared back. "What did *I* do to *her*? Gentlemen, I have had quite a morning. You may think to intimidate me, but I promise you, your threats are nothing compared to your quarrelsome sister armed with hot soup. Nor can you compare to my dear mother, who is the mistress of guilt and coercion. So let me tell you first and foremost that I have no intention of listening . . ."

"What did you do to make Grace cry?" said James,

also closing in on Adam, but with a less menacing demeanor.

"What did . . . what do you mean? She wasn't crying when she left me. She was probably laughing herself silly. I'm the one who should have been crying after she dropped the soup pot on my foot and burned me with boiling beef stock. Now, if you'll excuse me?" His attempt to get around the giants was blocked by the simple movement of one massive chest.

"Whether she let you see her cry or not, Mr. Havenhurst, Grace was crying and had been, all the way home, judging from her face. We don't like to see our sister upset like that, and you seem to be the cause."

"Me? Well, I . . . dash it all, that's one more thing for me to apologize for," said Adam turning away and shaking his head. "How much can she forgive? First my brother, then my mother, and then me. I don't have much hope, do I? Still I have to try. I was on my way to Dodwell Academy to apologize."

"I don't think Grace wants to see you," said David, using his chest to push Adam back against the staircase.

Adam's fist was caught by James's beefy hand, and he said, "I want to talk to the vicar alone for a minute, David."

"Very well. I'll wait outside."

"I noticed you limping," commented James when his brother had shut the front door. "Why don't we sit down and chat?"

"All right," said Adam, taking the straight Windsor chair and giving his visitor the sturdier easy chair. "I'm listening."

"I have to apologize. I forgot to give Grace the note last night."

"You . . . forgot?" said Adam.

"Yes, but I did give it to her afterwards."

"Unfortunately, I didn't know that," said Adam

glumly. Then he jumped up, slapped the heel of his hand against his forehead, and groaned. "So she could not have planned that fiasco with the girls! And I accused her of . . . devil take me, I've been an utter nodcock!"

"I can't deny that," said James, chuckling. "Not when you've made Grace cry. She never does so. I guess growing up with all of us, she learned that tears only proved you were a weakling."

"I have to talk to her, to beg her forgiveness," said Adam, striding toward the door.

"That's the ticket," said James, rising and clapping Adam on the back. "Just between you and me, I think Grace needs to get married. She's been running wild much too long, and we don't have the time to take her in hand. I mean, David doesn't want to, and I'm getting married myself soon, so I don't have the time."

James opened the door and motioned for his brother to come back inside. "We've straightened everything out, David. Mr. Havenhurst here is going to be our new brother-in-law."

Adam staggered back, wondering if he had heard correctly. He wanted to protest, to say that he would be the one to make such an announcement, even though he had come to the same conclusion earlier in the week. Seconds passed, and they watched him expectantly. Adam nodded, grinning like a want-wit. He allowed David to grasp his hand and crush his fingers while pumping his hand up and down.

"Let me go and harness my horse. I'll follow you back to the academy," he said.

"A capital idea, Mr. Havenhurst, or should I say, 'brother,' " said James, pulling David out the front door. "We'll wait for you."

Adam made short work of his task and was soon on the road to Grace's side. He found he was feeling much better as they drove along. Passing through the village of Pixley, the vicar was hailed by Richard Lambert, who was lounging against Miss Silverton's storefront.

"Good morning, Vicar," said the young dandy, putting one hand on the curricle as if to detain Adam.

"Good morning, Mr. Lambert. If you don't mind, I'm in a bit of a hurry," said Adam, nodding to the hand.

"I'm surprised to see you gone from home. I mean, I wouldn't have left if . . ."

Adam frowned, wishing he could consign the young man to perdition, but he was the vicar, and smiled patiently.

"If what?" Adam pressed. Just then, Grace's brothers rode into view and stopped beside the curricle.

"Oh, I thought Miss Edgewood was at your house, but I must have been mistaken," said Lambert, stepping back from the vehicle.

"So she was, along with her brothers. You do remember the Edgewood brothers, do you not?" asked Adam, taking pleasure in taunting the impertinent twit.

"Yes, yes. Good day to you, gentlemen," he said, taking to his heels.

Adam noticed that the other villagers, who had moments ago been loitering around the shops, also dispersed. He grinned, realizing how disappointed they must be to have him and Grace's brothers on such amicable footing. No doubt, when Grace passed through the village, they had assumed she was on her way to an assignation with him at the vicarage. They had probably been waiting all morning for the resolution. Good, he thought, it was just desserts for the nosy gossipmongers!

Grace had bathed her face and changed her carriage dress, which had suffered from splashing soup, for a soft wool morning gown of pale yellow. Since they had given the girls a holiday, she had nothing to divert her from her troubling thoughts, and she went to Uncle Rhodes's study for something to read. She was standing on the ladder to reach a novel on the top shelf when a soft whistle made her jump.

She turned her head and grimaced at the figure standing in the door.

"Good morning, Miss Edgewood. Mrs. Green told me I would find you here. May I help you down?" The Earl of Foxworth crossed the room and touched her elbow.

She jerked it away and snapped, "I can manage."

"I wonder if we might sit down," said the earl. "There is something very particular which I wish to say to you."

"You, too?" muttered Grace, ignoring the arm he offered and making her way to a single chair near the fire. "Whatever you have to say, my lord, say it quickly and then leave. I have no desire to bandy words with you, Lord Foxworth."

Alex lifted his brows, but he made no other comment. Instead, he sat down on a small table and possessed himself of her hand.

"I have spent the past week in mourning," he said.

"Mourning? I had no idea. Who passed away?" she asked, concerned despite her resolution to be cold.

"All my hopes and dreams," he said with a sigh.

Grace rolled her eyes and said coolly, "Now you are being foolish, my lord, and I have no time for foolishness."

"Do you not? I find being foolish is one of life's greatest diversions. But, I will desist since you do not enjoy it. Let me do you the honor of speaking plainly, Miss Edgewood."

"I wish you would," she said, tilting her chin and looking away.

"I have had several days, while I recovered from an, uh, indisposition, to consider our last conversation. I am willing to concede that you misunderstood my gift of the necklace. But you have had time to think, too. I meant no insult when I offered you the opportunity to be my mistress, but I can understand that you want more."

"My lord, this is getting ridiculous. I have no intention of becoming your mistress, and I resent the implication that I was merely holding out for higher stakes—your words, I believe."

The earl frowned, trying to recall when he had been foolish enough to use that term with Grace.

She explained quickly, "That is what your brother told me you said."

"Oh, yes, Adam. Well, as I was saying, although I think an offer to become my mistress is quite generous, I am willing to consider that, in order to have you in my bed . . ." He caught her hand in his as she doubled up her fist to darken his daylights. Holding both her hands captive, he finished in a rush, "I am willing to offer for your hand in marriage instead."

He released her hands and sat back.

Grace rose and paced the perimeter of the room, coming to a stop in front of him. Sitting on the table, his face was inches below hers.

"And what of love, my lord? You offer me marriage, but what about love? I have not heard a word about that."

He chuckled, and she balled up her fist, hiding it in the skirts of her gown.

"My dear girl, I am past such childish sentiments. Love has nothing to do with marriage. You really shouldn't read romance novels," he said, picking up the book she had taken off the shelves and giving it a condescending glance.

"So love and marriage have nothing to do with each other?" she said fiercely, drawing back her fist.

"Quite. Now as my mistress, there is the added excitement of lust," he said, placing his hands on her waist.

Grace tried to throw a punch, but he wrapped his arms around her, pinning her arms to her side and pulling her onto his lap. She closed her eyes and turned her head, her tactics causing him to chuckle.

"Soon you'll be begging for my embrace," he whispered.

The door crashed against the wall, and Adam flew across the room, grabbing Grace and pushing her into the chair before he flattened his older brother with one blow. Alex started up after him, then subsided when he saw Grace's brothers standing behind Adam. With a theatrical sigh, the earl slumped against Grace's feet, pretending unconsciousness.

"Adam, I . . ." What could she say? He had found her in his brother's embrace. He was probably past jealousy. He must be disgusted by her wayward behavior—so disgusted, he wasn't even bothering to scold her! That was not the man she knew and had come to love!

"James, you and David look after her. I'll take care of my brother," said Adam, helping Grace rise and turning her over to her brothers without addressing another word to her.

When the door had closed behind them, Adam prodded Alex with his foot and growled, "Get up, you coward."

Alex, gingerly touching his freshly injured eye, grinned unabashedly, climbed to his feet and shook his brother's hand.

"Thank you, Adam. You probably saved my life. I didn't fancy mixing it up with those two giants."

Extracting his hand, Adam said, "Get out of here before I forget I'm a vicar and finish the job."

"Adam, surely you're not going to hold this against me. I mean, you knew I had to try. Of course, if you weren't such a lobcock, you would have told me to go to the devil and leave your lady alone. That's all you had to do, you know."

"She's not my lady, and if I ever had a chance, after this morning . . ." said Adam wistfully. "I've been such a fool about everything."

"It's to be expected."

"Thank you very much," replied Adam.

"I mean, you haven't the reputation, and the experience it implies, to be able to handle the ladies. Becoming a vicar like you did, you never got past all that calf-love rubbish from your salad days."

"Well, I'm not likely to do so now. She'll never have me."

The earl put his hands on Adam's shoulders and said soberly, "If you do not declare your intentions to that girl before the end of this day, I will swear to the world that our mother played our father false, and that you are not my brother."

"And if Grace has any sense, she will turn me down," Adam said glumly.

"Devil a bit. You've just got to have the right approach. Now, let me think . . ."

"If you don't mind, Alex, I think I'll handle this one on my own, but for now, I'll let her get over your man-handling first."

"Yes, I thought that would do the trick," said the earl.

Adam's mouth dropped open, and then he grinned. "You don't think I'm going to believe that plumper, do you? I'm not your adoring little brother anymore."

"I swear on the Bible, your Bible, if you wish, that it was all part of my grand plan to get you and Miss Edgewood together. Why else would I offer carte blanche to a gently reared lady?"

"You're impossible," said Adam, but he was smiling as he followed his older brother out of the house.

* * *

When Adam returned to the vicarage it was to find a note asking him to call on Mrs. Odstock, whose mother had passed away that morning. The vicar of Pixley spent the remainder of the day, seeing to the details for the funeral services the next morning. After visiting with the family all day, night had fallen before he had the chance to return to Dodwell Academy.

He was torn between excitement and trepidation. He felt he was tottering on the edge between happiness and despair. One false move, and Grace would send him away, plunging him into a lifetime of loneliness. But if she said yes . . .

"Good evening, Mr. Havenhurst," said Rhodes Dodwell, ushering him into the drawing room, where James and David Edgewood were lounging on the sofa. Mrs. Stiles was seated at the pianoforte, playing a tune he didn't recognize. She smiled at him, and he felt better. Surely Mrs. Stiles, of all people, knew Grace's disposition toward him.

"Good evening, gentlemen, Mrs. Stiles," he said, shifting from one foot to the other. "Is Miss Edgewood at home this evening?"

"I'm afraid she is still indisposed, Vicar," said Mr. Dodwell. "The past few days have been very difficult for my niece."

"I see. Then I will not bother you further. Thank you, Mr. Dodwell. Good evening, everyone."

"Let me see you out, Mr. Havenhurst," said Mrs. Stiles, hurrying toward the door and taking his arm.

At the front door, she put her finger to her lips and followed him outside.

"Grace has gone to the bathhouse for a swim," she whispered, winking broadly at him.

"I see. Please tell her I'll call again tomorrow," said Adam, placing his hat on his head.

"No, no, you mustn't do that. I mean, you should put her out of her misery tonight, Mr. Havenhurst."

"I'm afraid I don't understand, Mrs. Stiles."

"Here," she said, pressing a key into his hand. "I will make certain there are no interruptions, just take care that you finish the job. Grace has been kept in suspense long enough, do you understand?"

"I think so," he replied, smiling down at the gray-haired lady. He took her hand and kissed it lightly, adding, "Thank you, Mrs. Stiles. You're a treasure."

Adam drove his curricle to the bathhouse and hopped down. The high windows were bright from the lamps burning in the wall sconces, but it was very quiet. He turned the key, letting himself inside noiselessly.

A lone figure was swimming at the far end of the pool. He watched for a moment, making sure it was Grace. She came closer, and he smiled. There could be no doubt it was she with those long, graceful limbs.

Taking a deep breath of courage, Adam stepped into the light and called her name. The swimmer stopped, then glided closer.

Holding on to the edge of the pool, Grace stared at him a moment before asking softly, "Aren't you afraid, Vicar, that you will be thrown out of the church for associating with such low company."

Adam squatted down. Touching her fingertips, he murmured, "If they haven't thrown me out for being a fool, then I am willing to take a chance—if you are, my dear."

"Adam, I have a confession to make."

"Oh?" he asked, stroking her cheek.

"Yes, I . . . I was not very honest with your brother. I was only trying to make you jealous, you know."

Adam chuckled, and said, "Then you should know that it worked like a charm, my love."

"My love?" she whispered. He bent down, and Grace arched her back to meet his lips.

She sighed. "That was lovely."

"Thank you," he said, his eyes twinkling in the firelight.

"Adam, there is one thing. I . . . I don't want to disappoint you, and I know you find me shocking at times."

"I can get used to it. As a matter of fact, I have grown quite fond of your shocking ways," he said, grinning at her.

He extended his hand to pull her out. Biting at her lower lip, Grace gave him an impish grin and grasped his hand firmly. Giving it a sudden yank, she pulled him forward, plunging him into the shallow pool.

Sputtering, Adam rose up and grabbed her. "You minx!" he exclaimed, pulling her close.

Grace squealed, but she made no move to escape. Throwing her arms around his neck, she kissed him with all the pent-up passion of a lifetime.

After several minutes, Adam drew back. Still holding her in his arms, he observed, "Yes, I think I could grow very accustomed to that, my love."

"Oh, Adam," she replied, giving herself up for another kiss.

Finally, he pulled away and climbed out of the pool, helping her out, too. Chuckling, he looked her up and down, from her pouting lips to her wool bathing costume.

"Looking at that, Grace, I really don't know why I ever worried about anyone seeing you or the other girls in their bathing costumes. No man could find such a hideous ensemble provocative."

Grace licked her lips and looked him up and down, her eyes resting on his soaked shirt. "But you, on the other hand, my dear . . ." She kissed the tip of his nose, and continued huskily. "Dear vicar, I find you very provocative in your bathing costume."

Adam's dark eyes widened in shock, and he opened his mouth to admonish her. Then he noticed her eyes were twinkling with laughter, and her lips were opened in the most kissable manner. Throwing caution to the wind, the vicar pulled his schoolmistress against his hard chest and proceeded to kiss her breathless once again.

Several minutes later, Grace leaned back in the curve of his arms and whispered, "And I intend to grow very accustomed to that, too, my love."

"Oh, I can guarantee it, my dearest Grace. I can absolutely guarantee it," he replied, matching the deed to his words.

About the Author

Julia Parks resides in Texas with her husband of thirty years. A teacher of high school French, she spends her free time writing, reading, and playing with her two grandchildren. She loves to hear from her readers. You may contact her through the publisher or by e-mail at dendon@gte.net. If you enjoyed this story, look for her next release, a Christmas story in which the Earl of Foxworth finally meets his match.

More Zebra Regency Romances

__A Taste for Love by Donna Bell $4.99US/$6.50CAN
    0-8217-6104-8

__An Unlikely Father by Lynn Collum $4.99US/$6.99CAN
    0-8217-6418-7

__An Unexpected Husband by Jo Ann Ferguson $4.99US/$6.99CAN
    0-8217-6481-0

__Wedding Ghost by Cindy Holbrook $4.99US/$6.50CAN
    0-8217-6217-6

__Lady Diana's Darlings by Kate Huntington $4.99US/$6.99CAN
    0-8217-6655-4

__A London Flirtation by Valerie King $4.99US/$6.99CAN
    0-8217-6535-3

__Lord Langdon's Tutor by Laura Paquet $4.99US/$6.99CAN
    0-8217-6675-9

__Lord Mumford's Minx by Debbie Raleigh $4.99US/$6.99CAN
    0-8217-6673-2

__Lady Serena's Surrender by Jeanne Savery $4.99US/$6.99CAN
    0-8217-6607-4

__A Dangerous Dalliance by Regina Scott $4.99US/$6.99CAN
    0-8217-6609-0

__Lady May's Folly by Donna Simpson $4.99US/$6.99CAN
    0-8217-6805-0

Call toll free **1-888-345-BOOK** to order by phone or use this coupon to order by mail.

Name_____

Address_____

City_____ State_____ Zip_____

Please send me the books I have checked above.

I am enclosing $_____

Plus postage and handling* $_____

Sales tax (in New York and Tennessee only) $_____

Total amount enclosed $_____

*Add $2.50 for the first book and $.50 for each additional book.

Send check or money order (no cash or CODs) to:

Kensington Publishing Corp., 850 Third Avenue, New York, NY 10022

Prices and numbers subject to change without notice.

All orders subject to availability.

Check out our website at **www.kensingtonbooks.com**.